GW00503699

Made in Heaven

Praise for Made in Heaven

*A wonderful love story in which the best of the
literary heroines, Jane Eyre, meets Bollywood.
I instantly loved Hema and thanked the author not
only for creating her, but also for making her so 'normal'.*
Sarah Ismail, Editor, Same Difference

*An honest and insightful look at the impact of a
tragedy on a family. A FINALIST and highly
recommended!*
**The Wishing Shelf Book Award 2020 for Where
Have We Come**

*[Saz] has a unique style of blending striking
themes with her favourite songs, giving the readers a gentle
feel of life and laughter.*
**Dr Pushpinder Chowdhry, MBE, Director, UK Asian Film
Festival**

About the Author

Saz Vora grew up straddling British and Gujarati Indian culture. Her books are stories that make you think, for readers who like the multicultural layers of South Asian family drama, Bollywood style gatherings and lots of references to food. She draws on her upbringing in England and the layers of complexity of living with her Indian heritage and her Britishness and uses this to create stories to represent that people from a diverse community with honest and positive life experiences.

Saz's debut novel in two parts was a finalist in The Wishing Shelf Book Awards 2020 and her short story *Broad Street Library* was long listed in Spread The Word Life Writing Prize 2020.

Please visit her website, where you can read her blog and sign up to her newsletter where she will share, missing scenes, recipes, playlists and all things book related.

Website **www.sazvora.com**

BY THE SAME AUTHOR

University Reena & Nikesh Duet
My Heart Sings Your Song Book One
Where Have We Come Book Two

All rights reserved. No part of this book may be reproduced in any form or by any electronic or mechanical means, including information storage and retrieval systems, without written permission from the author, except for the use of brief quotations in a book review.

This book is a work of fiction. Names, characters, businesses, organisations, places, events and incidents either are the product of the author's imagination or are used fictitiously. Any resemblance to actual persons, living or dead, events, or locales is entirely coincidental.

Note from Saz

The spelling used in this book is British which may be strange to American readers, but NOT to those living in Australia, Canada, India, Ireland or the United Kingdom. This means color is colour. I hope this is not confusing and will not detract from your reading experience.

The Gujarati words used in this book can be found in the Glossary at the back.

MADE IN HEAVEN

Copyright © 2021 by Saz Vora

www.sazvora.com

Author Photograph: Gulab Chagger

Print Book ISBN: 978-1-8381465-2-8

First edition. August, 2021.

10 9 8 7 6 5 4 3 2 1

For Kamlesh and my sons, I am who I am because of your love and support.
To Hassy

MADE IN HEAVEN

"When I saw this girl, she seemed to me like... like a glowing ray of light
Translated lyrics from, 'Ek Ladki Ko Dekha Toh'
Kumar Sanu, Javed Aktar

Soundtrack

To enhance your reading experience, you can listen to my soundtrack, search and scan on Spotify

Made in Heaven

ONE

AN ICY CHILL raced through my body as I focused on a pair of black beady eyes topped by shiny ebony hair. A memory stirred. Someone tugged at my pigtail, pushed me to the ground and laughed. My ears filled with the chanting, "Freak, freak, freak." I stared up at a dark-haired boy, his hands grubby with dirt. He formed a fist, and then pain, intolerable suffering. My legs thrashed and the children moved beyond my reach. I instinctively raised my knee to push my tormentor away, and he recoiled and bent double, holding his groin.

Except the boy had vanished. In his place stood a portly Sikh wearing a royal-blue turban and a high-visibility vest that fitted a bit too snugly. An empty plastic sack lay by his side.

I glanced around, finding myself in a train carriage instead of on an open playground. I must have fallen asleep. I'd dreamed that same, awful dream again.

I stood up and put my palm on the man's shoulder; his back curved as he nursed his wound. "Sorry... Sorry, Uncle."

He lifted his head. "No, no, my fault, my fault. I scared you, puttar." He pulled himself up, tentatively, and reached for the bag. I apologised again.

He held up his hand. "Yes, yes, I have to clean." He pointed towards the next carriage.

"Thank you for waking me up, Uncle." I yanked at my rucksack and overcoat, feeling sorry for the man I had hurt as a consequence of my nightmare, and flew out of the train. Jumping down onto the platform, I thrust my watch to my face. "Oh no, I'll be late. You stupid, stupid girl," I said under my breath.

"Wait. Wait, puttar."

I swung back at the voice behind me.

"Your book."

"Thank you, thank you." I tugged the novel out of the Sikh's grip and raced down the platform shouting, "Tusi great ho Uncleji, Sat Shri Akaal."

* * *

I FOLDED THE LETTER, put it back in the luxurious woven envelope and thrust it into my coat pocket. It had stayed in my job-hunting folder until I'd caught the train from St Pancras, and I'd resisted the urge to read it several times. But after the fright of being woken up and the build-up of dread in my stomach, I'd decided to read through the answers I'd pencilled in the margins again.

The job was to look after Amelie Amin, a four-year-old girl whose guardian, Rahul Raichura, was bringing her to England in September. If I got the job, I would be spending time in France until then, teaching her English.

At first, I'd thought it odd that someone who spoke Gujarati lived in France, but then I'd remembered watching a documentary about Ugandan refugees. When Idi Amin threw the Indians out of Uganda, many didn't have links to India or the UK. The people were dispossessed, stateless, and so many countries across the world had given them refuge, including France.

I peered at the tube map, counted the stations until my stop, then rummaged in my oversized handbag. The packed underground train heaved with people, their faces hidden behind brightly coloured images of a red steam engine and a boy with round, black-rimmed glasses. A greying woman with enormous spectacles that would have been fashionable in the eighties smiled at me as she stared at my book, leant forward, and declared, "This one's better, don't you think?"

I blinked in surprise. On my previous visits to London, no one had made eye contact, let alone talked to me. Mini, my cousin, hated the capital city. She was studying medicine at Imperial College because Dennis, her brother, attended LSE. But she repeatedly mentioned how soulless the city was, how even her neighbour didn't talk to her. She missed Preston and the friendly folk who said, "Ow do," as you walked down the street.

I mumbled a response and looked down at my book. Harry Potter and I were kindred souls. My name, Hemanshi Pattni, or Hema for short, meant we had the same initials. I wore NHS glasses, and until recently, a flesh-coloured Elastoplast had circled the nose bridge. I, too, lived with my aunt and uncle in a quiet cul-de-sac. My dastardly cousin was named Dennis. And I'd spent a good portion of my young life in the cupboard under the stairs, until Dennis's sister, Meenaxi, had developed Type 1 diabetes.

I loved Mini, that was my pet name for her. She kept me fed and cheerful, making up jokes and mimicking the two individuals who made my living at Beechwood Close almost unbearable. When she'd gone into hospital, my attitude had changed; I'd vowed to stop misbehaving and instead done everything my aunt had told me to do.

For a brief time, Mini became her mother's favourite child. My aunt maintained a diary of her food intake, assessed her blood sugars, took her to doctor's appointments. Life turned even more oppressive. My bothersome brother, Dennis, created mischief, and I lost the bubbly, happy sister I adored. Then Kalpesh Mama decided that Chanda Mami was treating their daughter like an invalid and insisted on taking care of all aspects of Mini's health.

Dennis, who could do no wrong, regained his status as the apple of his mother's eye and continued to create trouble for Mini and me. My cousin – his name was Dinesh, really, but everyone called him Dennis – gave me the first Harry Potter book as a joke.

"You have a lot in common with Harry, H.P.," Dennis said, as I held the book up, my eyebrows raised.

My shoulders tensed with disappointment and anger. My present for him was an expensive pen, and he'd given me a book. It wasn't my favourite genre, a stupid children's book. I envied Mini and her mother, who both had jewellery to adorn their necks. But that was my family. The only person who showed kindness to me was Mini. My uncle, Kalpesh, preferred a comfortable life, and his wife, Chanda, would berate and harangue him incessantly if she saw him give me any affection. He reminded me of water, always finding the most natural path to travel.

Another thing I had in common with Harry was a magical gift I'd discovered in the last term of junior school: languages. I had always picked up languages quickly and hadn't thought twice about speaking Gujarati, Hindi, Punjabi and Polish. It was only when my form tutor, Mr Hodgett, informed me I had talent after I had achieved the highest score in the French test that I started believing I was gifted.

Like Harry, I, too, had a scar from when my parents had died, but I hardly talked about it. Kalpesh Mama and Chanda Mami, my uncle and aunt, never spoke about that fateful afternoon. On the day Kalpesh Mama lost his sister, and best friend, and I became an orphan, my entire family perished, although Chanda Mami reminded me daily that I was lucky I had them.

TWO

I STARED AT the map as I stepped out of Richmond railway station. The announcement in *The Lady* called to me. A summer au pair job usually asked for English-speakers with some knowledge of French, Italian or German for families who summered in Europe. But this advert was unusual. It wanted an English au pair with knowledge of French and Gujarati, and when I'd talked to the woman on the phone, she'd switched between English and Gujarati to make sure I was genuine.

I reread the advertisement.

French-speaking Au Pair Plus required to teach English to a 4-year-old girl in South of France. The family will move to England and need their child to understand and speak English. As an Au Pair Plus, you will work 4 hours in the mornings and do some light babysitting, e.g. pickup from dance classes, etc.
Full driving licence and good recent references essential. Knowledge of Gujarati language helpful.

Richmond High Street was lined with boutiques and high-end coffee shops. I popped into House of Fraser to freshen up for the interview. The ladies' toilet had a full-length mirror. A quick touch-up of lipstick; a full turn to check that the slate-grey smart trousers and long-sleeved royal-blue shirt I'd changed into from my torn jeans and old sweat top were suitable. On the way out, I ran through the cosmetics department, spritzing some perfume from the counter. Every summer since I'd turned eighteen, au pair work had been my escape from my aunt's tirades. Last year, my full year abroad had made me realise how much I needed to distance myself from England and the obligatory visits to Preston. Being away had even reduced my nightmares.

The splendid Georgian-terraced house sat in a tree-lined square with Richmond Green – occupied by women, children and dog walkers – in the centre. I paused at the bottom of the steps leading to a painted red door, taking a moment to admire the face of the house covered with rows of tall windows. As I climbed the stone steps, I glanced down to the basement's modest courtyard, bordered with flowerpots. Trepid legs carried me up to the front door.

A dribble of sweat rolled down my back as I rang the bell. I rubbed my clammy hands on my coat as the wait stretched. Eventually, a plump, middle-aged Indian woman in navy blue trousers and a carnation-pink silk blouse opened the door. She held out her hand. Gayatri Raichura's layered shoulder-length hair parted to the side. Her eyes dimmed with sadness, yet her mouth smiled. She spoke English with the accent that only people who came from East Africa had. It reminded me of my mami's friends, who looked at me with sympathetic eyes.

I inhaled. *She doesn't know about your past, Hema.*

Inside, the smell of cut flowers infused the entrance hallway. An exquisite display sat like a squat deity on a round walnut table. Mrs Raichura asked me to follow her. The walls were painted in muted shades that only paint specialists could supply, and, as I approached the staircase, she took my coat and rucksack and hung them in a cloak cupboard.

"Can I get you some tea?" she inquired as we walked along a hall lined with a substantial gold-framed mirror and paintings of landscapes similar to work by Gauguin, Sérusier and Cézanne. I recognised a signature and shook my head. *They can't be originals, just excellent copies.* Gayatri looked over her shoulder and frowned. Had I said that out loud?

The formal sitting room had comfy sofas and chairs in subtle shades. It was littered with little shiny wooden tables filled with small trinkets and photo frames. The late afternoon sun streamed through the French doors that led to a terrace overlooking the garden. My eyes darted to the photographs. I clenched my fists, fighting the urge to snoop.

"Why are you desperate to get this job? Calm down, Hema," I whispered to myself. I tried not to think about why I wanted to be in France, how the money would allow me to travel in Europe. How I would do anything to lengthen my time away from Beechwood Close.

Gayatri Raichura placed a silver tray on the polished coffee table and sat down in the armchair. "It's English tea. Wasn't sure if you drink masala chai. So many young people don't nowadays."

"I... I drink masala chai." My words were raspy. I cleared my throat.

She leant across and patted my knee. "Don't be nervous. It is only a formality. Your CV and recommendations are splendid." She waited while I took a sip, then conducted the rest of the interview in Gujarati, asking about my hobbies and what drew me to work as an au pair in the summer. She explained that the girl, Amelie, had recently joined her family and that her son was the girl's legal guardian.

The telephone interrupted our conversation. I leant on the sofa, relaxing as I let go of my anxiety. Everything seemed to be going well.

"Hema, would you take this call? It's my son, Rahul. He wants to ask you a few questions." Gayatri held the cordless telephone out to me.

The voice was low and authoritative. "My mother tells me you match your impressive CV and references," he said in French.

These people are thorough. My heart thumped against my breast, the tension travelling to my shoulders. The man's tone made my nerves jangle; I had been too optimistic about getting the job.

I replied in the same language. The man on the phone emphasised that Amelie was the most important person in his life and that he wanted to make sure I understood my responsibility. I told him that none of the families I'd worked with had ever had complaints. Then he asked me a question which struck me dumb for a second.

When I responded, "I love it when my charges come to me shy and unwilling to talk at the beginning, but are confident by the end of the summer and don't even realise they are switching from one language to another," he seemed to relax.

"*Bonne réponse. Je pense que ca ira pour l'instant, mademoiselle.* Can you pass the phone to my mother? I would like a private conversation."

I sat while Gayatri Raichura went into the corridor to speak with her son. The words – *pour l'instant,* for now – buzzed in my head. Did the family have other interviews lined up? Before arriving, I'd been so confident the position was mine. *How many other people can speak both French and Gujarati?*

Mrs Raichura returned and informed me she would call me later, the dimple on her left cheek no longer visible.

My heart sank. *I haven't got the job.*

I had banked all my hopes on getting this job for the summer holiday and felt suddenly deflated, even though something about the way her son talked to me had turned my stomach. I rose abruptly, told her I needed to get to West London, and departed swiftly. Usually, I applied for at least three jobs, but after my telephone interview earlier in the week, I hadn't sent the other letters off. I'd have to remedy that mistake quickly – I had made a promise to never to return to Preston ever again.

***

AS I RAN TO THE STATION, more sweat trickled down my back, my rucksack adding to the weight in my belly. I fumbled with my purse to find a coin and listened for the payphone to connect.

"Hello, it's me. Just finished my interview." I tried to add some cheerfulness to my tone. A croupy sound came from the line. "Are you okay?"

"Yes… had to rush out of the bathroom. Congratulations." My cousin Mini's voice was breathy.

"I didn't get it. They said they'd let me know." Once those words fell out of my mouth, I was no longer upset, but annoyed. Gayatri Raichura and I had spoken on the telephone for an hour before the face-to-face meeting. She had implied that it was an informal chat to meet each other. I had even come down on the early train from Nottingham, the ticket dearer than the regular off-peak fare I would ordinarily have paid. My anger built to a crescendo. *She never mentioned she would need her son's approval.*

I banged my fist against the glass. "What a waste of my money and time."

"Ouch… tell me all about it when you get here," Mini said.

I squinted at my watch. "I won't be there at six, I'm still in Richmond."

"Don't worry; we don't need to be there until eight. Hey, Hems, chin up, plenty more jobs in *The Lady*," she chortled.

She was very secretive about what was happening that evening. The weight of the rejection lifted from my heart as I absorbed her excitement.

＜THREE＞

MY COUSIN LIVED in a house at the end of a row of semi-detached townhouses in Boston Manor, a suburb of Greater London. A white sign with sunny-yellow lettering hung above the entrance porch. There were three doorbells, one with 'Bright Smiles' engraved on a shiny metal plate. The other two were for the flats above. I pressed the doorbell and waited. Meenaxi Jogia, my cousin, opened the door. She was a head taller than me; her plump face beamed with an enormous smile. She wore a pair of slouchy harem pants and a baggy T-shirt. As soon as we entered the hallway, I hauled off my rucksack and hugged her.

She squeezed me tight. "Come on, I've made us khaman dhokla, and the chai's brewing."

I gripped her tighter. She was a great big sister. She'd known I would be upset and had prepared my favourite teatime snack. I told her I loved her.

Later, as I was drying off after a bath, Mini knocked on the bathroom door. "Phone call for you."

When I swung the door open, she waved the cordless handset at me. Frowning, I put the phone to my ear.

"Hema, It's Gayatri Raichura here."

I haven't got it, I thought. *I must have said something they didn't like.*

"Oh, thank you for letting me know... Good luck with your search," I replied, taking a deep breath.

"My search? Have you changed your mind? I thought we had a connection. How can I convince you to take the position? Is it the money? We can increase that. We'll reduce the hours. You can have the car on the weekend?" As she rattled off other benefits, it hit me. She had offered me the job.

My heart fizzed like a rogue firework and all I wanted to say was *thank you, thank you* a million times, but I refrained. "Sorry, Mrs Raichura, I meant, I would love to accept."

She let out a slow breath. "Good, good, I was... Never mind. Rahul will telephone you with the finer details. Are you contactable on this number for the rest of the week?"

Mini still stood in the hallway, her round inquisitive eyes roaming over my face, her lips lifted upwards. As she tugged me to her side, I said goodbye and switched the call button off.

"I knew you'd get it. How could anyone not give you a job? You're like the language whisperer. When the aliens land, they'll contact Hemanshi Pattni to help communicate."

Victory flooded me. We pranced around, laughing and jumping, until a knocking sound from the adjoining flat ended our celebration.

* * *

Kalpesh Mama and Chanda Mami waited for us outside the restaurant's door. My uncle and aunt were an unlikely pairing; he was six feet tall and skinny while she was four foot five and rotund. Every time I saw them standing together, her arm in the crook of his elbow, a nursery rhyme came to my mind.

Mini whispered, "And the dish ran away with the spoon," in my ear. My big sister had made the comparison before, and the image had stuck: the ridiculousness of a tall thin spoon and the round dish.

My throat tightened as my aunt studied my approach. I loved Kalpesh Mama, but Chanda Mami had pointedly informed me I wasn't part of her true family.

Strong arms pushed me and Mini apart from behind before we could reach my uncle and aunt. "So, girls, where are you going tonight, all dressed to the nines in your fine coats and high heels?"

Mini yelped. "Dennis, don't you know anything about women's self-defence? I was ready to garrotte you with this." She waved a long chain with a set of keys.

Dinesh Jogia was shorter than his younger sister. He had his mother's genes, the same tendency to carry weight and shortness.

"How are you, H.P.?" His dark mahogany eyes narrowed as he smirked.

I pressed my lips together. I would have feigned a headache if I'd known – anything to avoid this little family reunion.

Brother and sister exchanged a look, and Mini said quietly, "She got the job."

We locked arms and walked towards the ornate entrance.

"Dinu, Dinu, my dikro, I've missed you." Dennis's mother opened her arms in welcome, then held onto him for dear life, her head resting against his broad chest.

Kalpesh Mama hugged his daughter tightly as she rested her forehead on his shoulder. Then he pulled me into his arms, the familiar smell of his aftershave comforting me. His soulful gaze ran slowly over our faces, assessing our feelings, gauging our reactions to the mother-and-son greeting.

Chanda Mami cooed and asked after her favourite child's health. When she finished, her head bobbed at Mini and she asked in a cooler tone, "How are you, Meena, keeping well?"

In response, Mini stepped forward and pecked her mother on the cheek.

Dennis's mother reluctantly dragged her eyes away from her daughter and fixed them on mine. "Didn't expect you here. It's *our* family dinner. Shouldn't you be revising?" She spat the words out like stones.

My heart raced and my throat clogged as I kissed her, the sickly smell of her favourite perfume filling my nostrils.

"Hema had an interview today, Mummy." Mini glared as she stuffed her fists into her coat pocket.

Kalpesh Mama tucked me into his side and I sighed, already forgetting Chanda Mami's nastiness. I loved my uncle's hugs.

My aunt's lips pursed at her husband's gesture and her scornful eyes darted back to her son. "What is the speciality in this place, Dinu?"

Kalpesh Mama jutted out his elbows, and Mini and I slipped our hands into the spaces.

"Well, my lovelies, how are you two?" he whispered as we followed Dennis and his mother into the restaurant.

* * *

"I SHOULDN'T HAVE COME," I said as I stepped out of the toilet cubicle. "She's going to sulk all evening."

"You can't avoid her now that you're in your final year. What if you don't get work after the summer? You must go home; you can't stay in Nottingham forever."

I turned on the tap at the washbasin next to Mini and glanced at her face in the mirror. My cousin had the most beautiful eyes, with lashes so long they brushed against her manicured eyebrows. Her skin was flawless, the colour of milky coffee. She was pleasantly plump, since her restricted diet kept her weight in check. I was more like Kalpesh Mama – round face, small chin and copper-coloured, almond-shaped eyes. My skin still erupted in spots regularly, and I had a glaring red pimple on my little nose that I was trying to cover with concealer.

"I plan to find work straight away, that's why I went for the interview." I had hardly stayed in Preston since starting university. "Anyway, when you forced me to stay for two days over Diwali, she hated it. Do you remember what she did on my last day?"

Mini giggled. "Oh yes, I forgot about that. She thought you'd taken one of her Harrods facecloths. "Besharam! No one is going to marry you, putting that thing in… in… in there." Mini's tone precisely mimicked her mother's. She grabbed my shoulder. "Let's tell her you've got a job. That'll cheer her up, knowing you won't be moving back after your exams. She doesn't want me staying either."

A smile grew on my lips. "Yes, you're not Dinu either. Come on, let's get this over and done with. We should go clubbing tonight to celebrate my job offer."

* * *

BACK AT OUR TABLE, my mami sat sandwiched between her son and her husband. Dennis pointed to the vacant chairs on either side of him and his father. The waiter brought a bottle of Bollinger to the table.

"What are we celebrating?" Mini asked as we sat down.

Dennis grinned. "I got a job today, too."

Chanda Mami beamed. "You're such a clever boy. Isn't he clever, Kalpesh? Who's it with, Dinu?"

"I'll be an analyst for Morgan Stanley. I begin in September. So… H.P., what's your new job?" Dennis smirked. He was taunting me deliberately; he knew I had applied for a temporary summer position.

"Nothing as good as yours, Bhai. I have an au pair position in the South of France until the beginning of September. I start a week after my exams."

"That's not work." Chanda Mami put the glass of bubbly down. "I'm not saying cheers to that, it's babysitting."

"I'm sure Hema will get work, Chanda. You know she enjoys travelling," soothed Kalpesh Mama as he squeezed my leg.

"She had better find a proper job. All that education costs money."

I swallowed my champagne down in one gulp and concentrated on the tablecloth, focusing on the warp and weft with intensity.

Chanda Mami went on. "Do you have any idea what it has cost to look after you, Hema? You'd better find a job soon. We can't support you all your life."

"Mummy, please. Hema has a couple of interviews lined up this week, and they're with big banks, aren't they, H.P.?" Dennis added, kindness filling his gaze. Perhaps he hadn't mentioned the post just to make my life difficult. All my life Dennis had made mischief, goading his mother on, as she'd become more and more hateful. But at Diwali, he had been nice to me. A look of disdain grew on Chanda Mami's face as her favourite child sided with me.

Polite conversation occupied the table for the rest of the meal. My aunt and uncle spoke with their children about life and study, and I waited, displacing the remnants of my dinner on the plate. Eventually, Kalpesh Mama asked whether I was still on track for my first-class degree.

"You're like your mother, so ambitious and so hardworking," he said.

"She has to be, Kalpesh. Who else will support her?" Chanda Mami interrupted.

A lump developed in my throat, and I wished with all my strength that my parents were still alive. They would have asked after my health and wellbeing and been proud of their daughter.

My mami saw my head drop, and said, "But, if you can't find work, we are here to help you, Hema. After all, we are family."

FOUR

"HEMS, CALL for you."

The searing pain of moving my head was overwhelming as someone ripped the pillow from under me. I croaked, "What? Why would anyone call at this godforsaken hour?"

Mini put her finger to her mouth and whispered, "He can hear you." She pressed the phone to my ear.

A familiar baritone travelled to the pit of my stomach. "It's eleven o'clock, Ms Pattni. I believe that's not *too* early for a weekend."

"Is it?" *It's too early to call on a Sunday.* I took a breath. "Sorry, Mr Raichura, we had a late night, a... family reunion." My head throbbed from the lack of sleep and too much alcohol. Mini and I had rolled back to the flat at five in the morning after a night of dancing at Broadway Boulevard. The nightclubs in London were so much better than in Nottingham.

He sounded unconvinced by my explanation. "Are you at home for the next hour? I want to send the contract over by courier."

I was dumbstruck. This was a first, a contract for an au pair job sent by courier on a Sunday. I focused all my attention on what he was saying.

After hanging up, I found Mini in the kitchen, a small saucepan of chai brewing on the gas cooker. I slumped at the square Formica dining table, unable to breathe, the pit of my tummy aching. I had wanted this job so badly and had rested all my hopes on getting it, but I felt uneasy about Rahul Raichura. Just hearing his voice sent my senses into disarray. I cradled my pounding head in my forearms on the table.

MINI PROTESTED WHEN I DRAGGED her along to drop off the signed contract, but her presence comforted me. I dreaded that my new employer, the man who had my tummy in knots, would want to meet with me.

When Gayatri Raichura opened the door and led us to the sitting room, explaining her son was in New York, the uneasiness in my stomach settled. Mini's eyes roamed and widened, resting on the pieces of fine art distributed everywhere.

"My son collects art." Gayatri sat with a tray of snacks and masala chai. She poured the tea into teacups and asked us to help ourselves to the sugar. "He started when he got his first bonus and hasn't stopped."

I picked out the contract from my handbag and passed it to her; she took it and explained that it was only a formality that Rahul had insisted on. "We have nothing to hide, you understand, but privacy is something my son values highly."

The more I heard about Rahul Raichura, the more apprehensive I became. "What type of job does he do?" I whispered. In all the years I'd worked as an au pair, I had never had to sign a non-disclosure agreement. I knew that nannies sometimes did, but au pairs were young girls exploring new countries.

Gayatri raised her eyebrow. "Did you ask about his work?"

"Sorry, I didn't mean to pry; I understand your need for privacy. I can be very discreet."

"I'll let my son tell you if he wishes to, when he joins us. Your primary concern is to make Amelie's move to London as smooth as possible." Gayatri turned her gaze to Mini, who was stuffing her mouth with a whole chakri. "Meenaxi, what do you do?"

Mini covered her lips and gulped down the mouthful. "I'm studying medicine at Imperial College. Following in my father's footsteps; he's a consultant in plastic surgery at the Royal Preston."

Gayatri and Mini exchanged polite conversation while I tried to avoid looking at the photographs scattered in small frames around the room.

"I have some photographs to show you." Gayatri lifted a small album from a side table. The album featured shots of Amelie as a baby, chubby but tiny. Images of her as a toddler, on her first day at nursery, in playgrounds. Not one of her with her mother or father. *Have they adopted her from an orphanage?* The most recent photograph showed the little girl against a painted backdrop, wearing a pale blue dress, her chocolate-coloured hair in two pigtails, her red heart-shaped lips pouting at the camera and her cheeks rosy.

Gayatri handed me an envelope. In it I found a Polaroid of a small, thin woman barely taller than a teenager, her expression lifeless, holding a bundle in her arms outside a hospital. Nothing like the photograph you would expect of a mother with a newborn baby.

"This is Amelie's mother; she has passed…" Gayatri stopped.

"Oh… I'm so sorry," I said, and looked at Mini, who nodded in sympathy.

Gayatri took the picture back and walked to a small writing desk. She put the album and envelope in a drawer, locking it with a key from a keyring that hung from the waistband of her trousers. The ornate silver key holder reminded me of an ornament Chanda Mami added to her waist whenever she wore a saree, but Gayatri's had a set of actual keys on it. I recalled watching old black-and-white Indian films where the women had bundles of keys they would use to retrieve valuables from locked cupboards. I thought it was old-fashioned and was surprised to see Gayatri Raichura with such an accessory.

We discussed my travel arrangements in depth. I took down details of the address, and we left the house as the schools closed. Richmond was full of smartly dressed children in blazers and hats, chattering and playing as they made their way home.

* * *

"ARE YOU MEETING up with Gabriel?"

I smiled, but my gaze fell to my coffee cup. At least Mini had waited until I had sat down. I could tell by her mannerisms she was itching to ask why I was stopping off for a few days in Paris on the way to my new post.

She pried out the information as we lingered in the coffee shop. Gabriel and I had been seeing each other since November of last year. He was exploring Europe, and I was on my placement in France. Mini and I had no secrets, and I had told her we had continued to write. He had even spent part of the Christmas break with me, arriving on my birthday and staying until Boxing Day. When we'd spoken at Easter, we had both planned on meeting again, and my summer post in the South of France would be an ideal opportunity. Our plan was a brief catch-up before I started, followed by a lengthy holiday at the end of September, before I came back to England and Gabriel returned to Canada.

"You've seen his photo," I sighed. "He's like a Greek god. He won't be in Europe for long. I think he just misses talking with me."

"You shouldn't listen to Mummy. You're stunning, Hema. So what if you're dark-skinned? It's her prejudice, not yours." Mini reached for my hand.

"Yes, and my back. What about that?"

Furrows appeared on her forehead. "Have you spoken to your group lately?"

"Been busy lately, but I'm speaking to them this week." I lifted the coffee cup to my lips. I preferred not to talk about my support meetings. I appreciated her concern, though. After all, it was Mini who had put me in touch with a therapy group – all of them dealing with a loss, all of them coping with visible signs of damage.

FIVE

I WAITED PATIENTLY at the bus stop. I had told Gayatri Raichura that I would make my own way to the house, but she had insisted that the housekeeper would pick me up.

A gaunt woman with a dark, severe haircut and a card stating 'Hema Pattni' approached the waiting group who had assembled by the exit, most of them chattering teenagers on summer holiday. I stood by the side of the door and raised my hand to grab her attention. When I spoke, she ignored me until I switched to French, then she introduced herself as Céleste Deveraux.

It felt good to be back in France. The year before, I had spent six months in Paris working for a hotelier as part of my placement. That was where I'd met Gabriel – handsome, olive-skinned, blond-haired. He, too, had staffed the reception desk. We'd continued our relationship after I'd returned to England; we had discussed the option to break up, but he had wanted to carry on seeing me, even if we lived in different countries. When I caught the train to Aix, my chest ached; I couldn't believe someone as good-looking as Gabriel wanted to be with me.

"Madame Raichura has instructed me to take you home; she and Amelie are with Monsieur Graux this afternoon."

When I slipped the odd word of English in my conversation, which was becoming increasingly common in French society, Céleste sneered at me with the disdain that only the French could muster. The English and the American expected everyone to speak their language. But the French expected all educated people to know French.

* * *

AMELIE SKIPPED UP TO ME, wrapped her arms around my neck, and gave me a wet kiss on my cheeks. She was small for a four-year-old. Her features were doll-like, tiny but in perfect proportion. She wore a white cotton dress with embroidered yellow daisies, her chocolate-coloured hair hanging to her waist.

"Bonjour, Amelie, what a lovely greeting. I'm sure we'll be best friends." I handed out the gifts I always brought for my families. "These are for you."

"Ooh, ooh." Her lips formed a perfect heart. *"J'adore des cadeaux, Mademoiselle Pattni*. I love presents, don't I, *Mémé*?" She translated her French to Gujarati for Gayatri and clapped her hands. Céleste brought lemonade to the sitting area and stood discreetly behind us.

The child's little fingers tore at the paper. She lifted the small box and enquired, "What is this called in English?"

"A telephone box."

"And the car?"

"That's a London taxi," I answered, smiling, and my heart swelled.

"Ooh, a red bus. Is this from London, too?"

"*Oui*, that is a bus," I replied.

She repeated the words, rolling them in her mouth to familiarise herself. "Bus... bus... ooh, that's like bus bus." She giggled at the joke; the words meant 'just enough' in Gujarati.

I liked her straight away; she was inquisitive and outgoing, switching from French to Gujarati without hesitation.

Gayatri Raichura's frown lines smoothed. "What do you want to eat today, my ladli dikri? Céleste is waiting. Pizza, pasta or dall, baath, shaak?"

Amelie turned to me. "What would you like to eat, *Mademoiselle*?"

"I think you can call me Hema. We are friends, you know."

"Ema, Ema, is that a Gujarati name?"

I chuckled at her pronouncement, "No, it's Hema. It begins with an aitch."

"Ema, Ema, I can't say it." Her face scrunched up and her bottom lip quivered.

I pulled her towards me as my heart squeezed. "Ema it is, then. Don't you think Ema is a better name for me, Masi?"

"Haan, I like Ema, too. Ema, what would you like to eat tonight?" Gayatri's lips curled up, her eyes drifting to Amelie, who sat on my lap.

"Can I have shaak and rotli, please? I haven't had that for so long."

We ate our evening meal on the veranda. Amelie asked questions in between mouthfuls, pulling at the rotli with both hands and eating her shaak with a spoon.

Céleste sat with us, too. She wasn't just the housekeeper.

I had been with other families where the housekeeper ate alone in the kitchen, never blurring the boundaries. As an au pair, I ate with my charges and occasionally ate with the family. Gayatri explained that they wanted me to be part of the family. As for Céleste, there was an aloofness in her manner towards me. I knew I would have to make an extra effort with her, especially with caring for Amelie.

* * *

ONE MORNING AS WE WERE exploring the woods, naming all the creatures and flowers in English, Amelie told me her mother had taught her the Gujarati names. "When I saw *Maman* after dance class yesterday, she said I'll be with her soon. Can we draw instead today?"

I stopped, taken aback. *Doesn't she know of her mother's death?* "But you're so clever, my little girl. You can already speak English. It would be great to show her." I made a mental note to talk with Gayatri about what Amelie had said.

SIX

UPON OUR RETURN, news from Gabriel pushed my concerns about the little girl to the back of my mind.

I reread his letter repeatedly, unable to control the remorse that filled my heart. I forced cheerfulness when with the family, but in the evening, instead of staying on the deck reading a book, I went for a long walk up to the reservoir, unable to grasp what Gabriel had written.

I replayed every conversation we'd had about meeting up for our holiday in September. The days in Paris together had been blissful. When I'd left him at Gare de Lyon, he had comforted me and told me he loved me. *What changed? Why did he write that letter?*

I slept fitfully that night, unable to let go of his memory. Then again, it had all been too good to be true. *How could someone as perfect as Gabriel love me? I'm imperfect.*

The night took forever to end, and in the early hours of the morning, I became angry at his deception. The meeting in Paris had not been as I'd thought. *It was a breakup session, a way to end it all.*

Flipping on the light, I reread the letter. *I can't do this anymore, Hema, this long-distance relationship thing doesn't work for me.*

His slanting script burnt into my eyes.

* * *

THE NEXT DAY, I woke with a heavy heart and lit a divo in the little family temple. It was the anniversary of my accident, and Gabriel's letter added to the misery that settled like a boulder in my stomach. I rubbed away scalding tears and stepped outside for a walk up the path through the woods.

A woman spoke with Céleste by the garden gate. At my approach, they broke apart, and the stranger's tiny, darkly dressed figure scurried up the trail before I reached her. Céleste bid me good morning, scorn on her thin face, and marched back towards the house. She usually introduced me to people she knew, even if she loathed to mention that I was the Raichuras' au pair. But I ignored the sourness of the exchange. I was hurting too much to worry about it.

After my walk, before heading down for breakfast, I reached for the concealer to deal with the dark circles under my eyes and the red rawness on my nose. Downstairs, I found the family at the dinner table, Amelie chatting to her grandma in Gujarati, dropping the odd English word into the conversation. Like me, she had a gift for languages, and the throbbing ache in my heart eased. I was proud of the little girl and how well-adjusted she was. I recognised how challenging dealing with change could be. For me, it had been extended stays in hospital, my memories blurred by the sedatives that had surged in my bloodstream. Even now, I still remembered the hurtful pain of exclusion because of my disfigurement.

As I headed to the kitchen for some water, my glass slipped out of my grasp and shattered into pieces. As I studied the scattered shards, my eyes burnt. A watery film blurred my vision, obscuring the broken glass.

Gayatri rushed to my side, her keys jangling my fragile nerves and crouched down to help pick up the mess.

"I'm sorry, I'm really sorry, I'll pay for the replacement." Suddenly the sobs I'd been trying to control escaped and wouldn't stop. I squatted against the cupboard, hardly noticing the fragments of glass that lanced into my palm as the well of tears overflowed.

Gayatri looked troubled by my reaction. "Now, now, it's only a glass. I can get another, accidents happen."

I looked at her, stood up and rushed to my room. I didn't want her pity; what did she know about me? I hated the kind words and sympathetic expressions. How could anyone understand? They had no sense of my life. Of the everyday reminders that I was the only one who had survived.

Why me? I'm not special. Why did they all have to die? To this day, I saw the sadness when my mama remembered his sister, his only family. And most of all, I observed how he would stop in mid-conversation when he recalled his early years in England when he'd found his best friend, Kartik, my father.

Gayatri knocked on the door. "Can I come in?" The door creaked; the mattress dipped as she sat on the bed.

I mopped my face with my sleeve and sat against the headboard.

"Tell me, what happened to you, today? You've been sad since your morning walk."

"It's the day of the accident."

"Accident?" she asked.

"My family all died today," I gulped out.

There was a sadness about Gayatri Raichura. It was the first thing I'd noticed when we met. Even here in sunny France, she had days when the smiles for her granddaughter hid a melancholy. I sensed she would understand. Her eyes mirrored mine.

She pulled me towards her and apologised. I couldn't hold back the sobs again, the constant grief of being besieged by my memories. The longing and ache for the family I had never known swept over the dam I had built. She stroked my hair and caressed my back.

"What's the matter with Ema, *Mémé*?" Amelie stood at the door.

I wiped the tears with my palms as she tentatively approached the bed. "Come here." I patted my lap, and she climbed into it. "I just need a cuddle."

"Ooh, is that all? I can give you lots of cuddles. *Tonton* tells me I give the best cuddles, don't I, *Mémé*?"

"Yes, Rahul says you give the best cuddles and kisses, ladli dikri."

"Why don't you make Ema your dikri? Did you know she doesn't have a *maman* or *papa*?"

A smile took over Gayatri's face. "Okay, come on my dikri, time for games."

Amelie clapped, jumped off the bed and ran to the door. "Are you coming, *Mémé*, Ema?"

I blew my nose and smiled at Gayatri. "Yes, give me some time to freshen up. You choose what we're playing."

After Amelie had gone, Gayatri squeezed my shoulder. Her eyes drew an arc on my face. "I know it's too soon, but will you tell me about the accident and how you got those scars on your back, Hema? Sometimes it helps to talk about these things."

I frowned at her. *How does she know about the scars?* I was always so careful to hide them. Even my swimming costume was the kind of one-piece Olympic swimmers wore, the high back covering the severe scarring and telltale marks from the skin grafts. I had kept underwater in the pool and used my towel to cover my shoulders before I'd climbed out. I fiddled with the floaty long sleeves on my dress to avoid her gaze.

"I'll meet you on the deck, dikri. It's a glorious day; we can't play indoors today." She kissed my cheek and left the room.

SEVEN

"WHAT ARE YOU doing?" I asked Amelie as I walked into the TV room after our English lesson.

"Dance practice." She rummaged through a drawer and picked out a DVD case. She turned on the TV and popped the disc into the player. The menu was in French, and she scrolled through to the songs from *Kuch Kuch Hota Hai*. "Do you want to join me?"

When my jaw dropped, she said, "*Ça va,* hu tamane batavis, mara *Tonton pense que je suis un excellent professeur de danse.*" She switched between French and Gujarati. 'It's okay, I'll show you; my uncle says I'm an excellent dance teacher.'

Amelie selected a song. "Do you know this?"

I nodded. Mami was a big fan of Bollywood films, and when we were younger, we had often gone to the cinema as a family. But as we'd grown, neither Mini nor I had continued, though Dennis had talked incessantly about the recent film releases.

"So, I'll be Tina and you can be Anjali; *Tonton* is Shah Rukh." She clapped her mouth shut, her eyes wide. "No, I can't be Tina, she marries Rahul… Rahul is my uncle." After a moment of thought, she said, "You can be Tina, I'll be Anjali."

My stomach fluttered. Just the mention of Rahul's name affected me. I had hoped that Rahul's work delay meant I would not meet him in person, but Gayatri had told me this morning that Rahul was due to arrive from New York soon. The apprehension of meeting him had sent my senses into overdrive.

Amelie choreographed a dance that copied all the movements by the three leads, clapping the rhythm as I followed her steps. We danced for at least an hour, Amelie instructing me to move my hips like Rani Mukerji. I fell, exhausted, on the small sofa, and Amelie climbed onto my lap, her thumb in her mouth, as we watched the film for the rest of the morning.

Céleste came in with snacks and drinks and reprimanded Amelie for sucking her thumb. I had observed how the two adults insisted that she stop. It upset me, as I remembered how much comfort I'd got from doing it when I was younger. The more time I spent with the child, the fonder I became of her. She was cheerful and happy. *What harm can a bit of thumb sucking do?* I decided that as soon as her grandmother came back from her walk with Phillipe Graux, I would raise the subject.

Amelie was telling me that Shah Rukh Khan was the man of her dreams, and she wanted to marry him, when Gayatri came into the room.

I laughed. "Isn't he too old for you?"

"He's not that old, Ema. I know when he meets me, he'll want to marry me." She knitted her brows together, her chestnut eyes focused on mine. "Do you have someone you want to marry, Ema?"

"No, I'm too young for marriage. As are you, little girl."

"You can't marry yet, ladli. You're coming to live with me." Gayatri sat down next to us. "So, has little Anjali found big Anjali yet?"

We continued to watch the film. I had seen it once before when Dennis had insisted we have a Bollywood screening during the holidays. Because I already knew what happened, my mind kept wandering, and I spent most of the movie wondering at what Rahul Raichura looked like. There had been photographs of him in the many picture frames at the house in Richmond, but at the time, I had been too apprehensive to look. My imagination was creating an image, building a picture of him. I pictured a honed body, a face as intimidating as his voice, his eyes dark and brooding. In my mind he was nothing like Shah Rukh Khan, but more like Tony Montana from Scarface.

✳✳✳

I WAS ENJOYING MY STAY in France and had even found a small language class where I could teach English. That evening, I had arranged to meet with them for supper and conversation. I walked toward town, enjoying the stroll down the scent-infused country lane.

I didn't see the shimmering sports car turn into the dirt road until the last second; nor did the driver see me. I jumped out of its way and landed in the bougainvillaea. The vehicle stopped at a distance.

"Are you hurt? I'm so sorry," the driver shouted as he ran up to me.

My sight adapted to the dim light. When I'd left the house earlier, the sun had been setting, but now it had disappeared entirely. The waning crescent moon pulled the road into complete darkness. Only the car's lights pierced the night as a man squatted in front of me, his dark gaze exploring me for signs of injury.

"Did I hurt you?" he repeated.

He helped me stand up, his heated hand clasping mine. I tested my ankles one at a time and checked for any aches and pains, then shook my head as I looked up at him. The warmth of his body made my chest tighten.

"Can I take you home, *Mademoiselle*?" He spoke French with an accent that told me he was not a resident of Provence; it was Parisienne, but there was something else in it I couldn't quite place.

I replied that nothing important was broken, just my pride, and admired his face. His eyes were small and pointed downwards. His hair was swept back, and when he spoke, deep creases appeared on his cheeks. I would have liked to have met this fine Gaelic gentleman in another circumstance.

"*Je suis vraiment désolé*; it would be my honour to take you back to your home." His rich voice permeated through my body.

"Get a grip, Hema," I mumbled under my breath.

"Sorry, did you say something?" he asked in French as he picked up my handbag.

I smoothed my hand over my long floaty dress, shaking off the dirt, and looked up to him. "*Non, non, Monsieur. Vous êtes trop gentil.*" I told him I was meeting friends at Jacques's, a small family-run restaurant across the major road.

He rubbed his chin. The stubble made a rasping noise, and when he smiled, his perfectly even teeth threw my insides into turmoil. I lifted a hand and said goodbye, then turned to walk away as elegantly as I could. He was far too old for me, his eyes far too serious. Then it dawned on me that I hadn't thought about Gabriel for days. I turned my head. The stranger was still watching, one hand holding his elbow, the other clasping his jaw. His fingers raked through his hair, cupped his neck, and he turned back to his car.

Have we met before? There was something familiar in that action and the voice, the cadence. *What's the matter with me? I must stop this daydreaming.*

EIGHT

THE MORNING AFTER Gayatri's comments about my scars, I wore one of my baggy T-shirts over my swimming costume for my early morning swim. No one needed to know how I'd got the injuries; they had been with me for most of my life, and I had tried my best to keep them safe from prying eyes. After climbing out of the pool, I pulled off my swim cap and loosened my hair. I grabbed my thin linen gown, put on my glasses and hesitantly approached the man sitting at the table. When I had started my swim earlier, nobody had been sitting on the veranda. The man must have been a near neighbour who had come to pick up Gayatri.

"*Bonjour, Monsieur.*" I held out my hand. So far everyone I had met was French. He lowered the newspaper that had shielded him.

"Good morning, Hema. Pleased to meet you, finally." Rahul Raichura stood up and clasped my hand. The picture I'd built up of him was nothing like the man in front of me. His slender form was taller, and his eyes didn't brood, but twinkled. He wore two collared t-shirts and a pair of beige shorts instead of the dark suits I'd imagined.

Even more surprising, it was the man I had met the night before. He hadn't looked Indian in the dark, maybe because his nose was smaller and upturned at the tip. Nor was his skin the same walnut hue as mine – but then again, his mother's complexion wasn't dark either. I, on the other hand, had the dark tones my aunt loathed.

His hot hand was still holding mine when Amelie rushed up and gripped his legs. "*Tonton, Tonton, Mémé* said you were coming! I went to sleep, and you are here."

His dark, intense gaze fell to his niece. He knelt. "*Ma pitchounette*, my cutie. Haven't you grown? Come here, my dikri." He spoke in French, English and Gujarati, and gave her a tight hug.

Amelie turned her head up to me, her eyes beaming. "Ema, *Tonton* is here. Now we'll have the best time."

"Ladli dikri, your hot chocolate is ready," Gayatri shouted through the kitchen window.

Rahul smiled back at me as Amelie pulled him into the kitchen. I liked his smile. It filled his face and made tiny lines appear at the edges of his eyes. My chest tightened and my legs hollowed. On the phone, his dealings with me had been professional and aloof, but in person, this man was warm and friendly.

"Stop this, Hema; he's your employer," I told myself quietly.

***

RAHUL RAICHURA HAD ASKED ME to join him for a walk so we could get to know each other better. My first instinct had been to decline, to have a conversation in the house, but his mother insisted that I take him up on the offer. She said Rahul knew some amazing places to see around Aix-en-Provence and that she'd arranged a play date for Amelie. So I reluctantly agreed to his request. Many of my families had done this, but there was something about him that put me on edge.

I watched him pace in the hallway, his hands held behind his back, sunglasses perched on his sleek hair. He had changed into a pair of beige chinos and was wearing a collarless pale-pink linen shirt with a white T-shirt underneath. He drew a leisurely stare up my frame, and my stomach clenched. I made myself concentrate on my feet as I climbed down the stairs.

"Good, it can get windy at the barrage." A slow smile appeared on Rahul's face.

My legs weakened, my breath halted, my stomach sank to my feet. I adjusted the strap on my floral dress and pulled at the sleeve of the T-shirt underneath, but only to stop myself from staring at him. The night before, in the dim light, his hair had shone in places, and I'd thought then that my eyes were playing a trick. Now, though, I realized that specks of grey peppered his dark brown hair. I wondered how old he was. His mother didn't look a day over fifty.

We walked towards the double garages by the side of the house; the doors opened automatically to reveal two vehicles: a red Peugeot 206 and a gold BMW 3-series convertible. The same car that had pushed me into the bush. Rahul strode to the BMW's passenger side and held the door for me. As I turned to look up at him, my stomach rose and smashed against my ribs. A slight twitch appeared on the edge of his lips. Settling in the seat, I glared at the dashboard and waited for him to climb in. He cleared his throat and slid into the driving seat.

"Let me show you the *locales.*" He reversed out of the garage, placing his right hand on the back of my seat. My neck felt the heat from his arm.

A few minutes later, we pulled over for Céleste's car to pass on the narrow drive, then continued on.

"I thought… you were a… a glowing ray of light." Rahul's head turned from side to side, the rimmed tortoiseshell sunglasses shielding his expression.

My throat tightened as I wondered why he'd said those words. "What does that mean?" I mumbled under my breath.

A thin smile twitched on his face. His cheekbones were prominent, and his greying sideburns gave him a distinguished air. When he twisted his head towards me, I looked away.

"Your CV is very impressive, Hema. I'm assuming summer au pairing isn't your ambition in life?"

I blinked. I'd only met him this morning, and already, he was asking what I planned to do with my future. My entire body tightened. *What does it matter if I wish to be an au pair?* It was a job that needed doing for people like him. I knew it was a *bête noire* for my mami, but I loved to travel, and what better way to do that than as an au pair?

I inhaled. *Calm down, deep breaths, Hema.* Rahul had every right to determine whether I was responsible or would go off as soon as things got complicated. I'd seen families and au pairs part company many times.

I sighed and started my pitch. "My ideal job would be in finance and languages." I explained that I wasn't looking for more work this summer but was planning to go to Eastern Europe.

"Why Eastern Europe?" His voice travelled through my ears and settled in my chest. He made me nervous.

"I want to go before the tourists ruin it. And I want to pick up a few of the languages."

"Your family doesn't mind you travelling alone?"

My body heated and I stared at my clenched fists. "My parents died in a car crash when I was two."

He changed hands on the steering wheel and placed his arm briefly on the back of my seat. My heart skipped.

He angled his head towards mine. "So sorry, Hema."

He flipped the sun visor and removed a CD. "Ek ladki ko dekha toh aisa laga" came through the speakers. It was from the film *1942: A Love Story*, one of Chanda Mami's favourite Bollywood movies.

Rahul had quoted a song lyric at me. The heat of the sunlight warmed my body further as we drove up the long winding road to the reservoir. I had walked up the forest path plenty of times but had never come up the road. The view was breathtaking.

***

"THE LIGHT IN THE SOUTH OF FRANCE is so vivid," Rahul finally said as we stopped halfway across the bridge. "That's why you see so many people here." He gestured to the easels and artists dotting the park, then pulled off his sunglasses and turned until his body aligned against my side. "Have you been to the Musée Granet in Aix?"

A slow tremble ran down my back as I turned to face him and told him it was on my list of places to visit.

"Don't go without me," he said, his voice carrying through every cell. The timbre lingered in my body and took up residence. "Do you appreciate art, Hema?"

I walked to the railings and stared at the water, watching the sun dance on the ripples as the currents pulled. The slow churn reminded me of the dangerous currents of attraction growing within me.

Suddenly, a gust of wind lifted my hair upwards. My three-quarter sleeved T-shirt covered my arms, but without the screen of my hair, my low neckline would reveal my back. I turned; the wind's gust pushed my curly locks down. Rahul strode in front of me and walked backwards.

His mouth lifted. "Is your hair naturally curly, or do you use tongs?"

"All natural, I'm afraid." I pulled at a tendril and continued towards the other side of the valley. When I glanced back, his expression had closed off. There was no sign of the teasing, twinkling eyes.

What have I said to offend him? I'd only told him my hair was naturally curly. My nails dug into my palms; my anger built. He shouldn't have volunteered to take me on a tour if I bothered him so much. "Take a breath," I muttered to myself.

He stopped. "Sorry, did you say something?"

"No, no, it's beautiful here. I came to Montpellier last summer, but Aix-en-Provence is beautiful; the town and the surroundings are stunning."

He nodded. "It *is* beautiful here. I bought the house because of the light. It's a wonderful place for relaxing. Will you find work after your travels in France or are you set on returning home?"

I relaxed a little; perhaps the mood swing was related to jetlag. I told him of my plans to return to London. How I had already sent off some applications and I was not averse to working in Europe. He listened, nodding in all the right places. I became comfortable in his presence, my heart returning to its normal rhythm as I spoke of how much I loved France and how I would love to live here eventually.

His head tilted and his lips lifted as he held out his hand and we climbed up the escarpment. There was a small clearing where many stood to gaze at Mount Victoire in its full glory. Our shoulders bumped. I stepped away but twisted my ankle and yelped. He pulled me to his chest, stiffened and pushed me back.

Our return journey to the house passed in silence. When we arrived, Rahul could not get away from me fast enough. Jumping out of the car, he yelled a "thank you" as he ran upstairs to his office.

NINE

THE NEXT MORNING, as I strode out to the patio, Gayatri said, "Can you pick up Amelie from dance school, Rahul?"

He folded his newspaper slowly, the sun magnifying the specks of grey in his wet hair. "Why, what's Céleste doing, Ma?"

"When will you listen to me? I told you Mukesh is coming today." She picked up his plate and went back into the kitchen. Rahul pushed his chair back to follow her.

As I approached, Rahul nodded a greeting and stepped aside. Inside the house, Gayatri loaded the sink, plates clanking into the porcelain basin.

"Sorry, Ma, do you want me to get him?" Rahul said.

"No," she replied as I watched her through the open window. "I want to. Can't you pick up Amelie? Are you that busy?"

"I wish you would drive in France, Ma. The car just sits in the garage and Céleste can't chauffeur you everywhere. She has responsibilities. Why don't you get Hema to fetch Amelie?"

"It's Hema's afternoon off. Besides, she has lunch plans," she sighed. "Don't worry, I'll take a cab."

"No, no, I'll pick up Amelie." He kissed his mother on the cheek as she continued to wash up. "Come on, Ma, please forgive me."

Gayatri spun towards him, her keyring jangling at her waist, and splashed water at her son. He blinked, then a grin grew on his face. His gaze met mine through the kitchen window.

I dropped my eyes to my plate, unable to breathe or swallow.

* * *

SEBASTIEN GRAUX SAT NONCHALANTLY at the little table on the terrace of Café Moritz. I had seen a photograph of him, but he was better looking in the flesh, with his chestnut-brown wavy hair, high cheekbones, square face, and bronzed skin.

I introduced myself, speaking in French.

He looked up. "Good afternoon, Hema, I am... *comment dit, ravi de vous rencontrer...*"

"Pleased to meet you, *on dit*; pleased to meet you," I replied.

Phillipe Graux, a neighbour of the Raichuras, had heard about my conversation classes and asked me to tutor his nephew Sebastien, who was spending a year in England as part of his business course. He had the Gaelic charm of his uncle, and we fell into conversation quickly. He knew English but was uncertain of his pronunciation. I told him everyone in England loved the French accent, the melodic tone and the sophistication of the language, and he leant forward and relaxed.

When it was time to pay the bill, I took out my purse, but he insisted on paying. His cornflower-blue eyes twinkled as he grabbed the receipt.

"No, no, Hema, this one is on me." He raised one neat eyebrow. *"Comme ca?"*

I laughed and watched him walk into the restaurant.

"Hello, Hema."

That voice. My stomach lurched.

When I looked up, Rahul stood over me. He pulled back the chair Sebastien had just vacated, placing his shopping bags on the ground.

"Where's your lunch date?" His sulky gaze roamed my face, sending a burning sensation coursing through my body.

"Bonjour monsieur…" Sebastien approached, looking questioningly in my direction.

"Sebastien, English, please," I rebuked.

"Pardon, Hema. Sir, how can I help you?"

Rahul introduced himself and pulled at a nearby chair, but Sebastien shook his head and stood.

"I have heard a lot about you, Mr Raichura." Sebastien held out his hand.

There was a brief conversation between them, on each other's families and the tennis club they both belonged to. All of it in English with the odd French word.

I beamed at Sebastien. He wouldn't need too many conversational English sessions with me.

"I have to go, Hema." Sebastien leant to kiss both my cheeks. "I have an appointment this afternoon. I'll call you."

Rahul's brows furrowed as he watched the exchange. "Please stay for a coffee?" he asked me as he waved to a waiter.

My initial reaction was to excuse myself. The walk at the reservoir had confused me, his mood swings unpredictable. When I looked up, his eyes had softened and fine lines had appeared at the edges. My resolve softened, too, and I agreed to stay a little longer.

We spoke of Amelie's progress, and he complimented me on how I'd engaged her in learning the language.

"Can I ask a huge favour?" he said after we'd exhausted the subject of his niece's English. "Will you come with me to pick up Amelie from dance school?" He raked his hair, and a soft chuckle escaped from his mouth. "I'm a bit nervous, never done this before."

* * *

RAHUL OPENED THE CAR DOOR for me. Nobody opened doors for anyone anymore. It was so old-fashioned. But then again, he was at least ten years older than me.

At the dance school, a crowd had gathered at the pickup area. I introduced Rahul to the mothers, au pairs and housekeepers. He politely asked about their children, all the while building an awareness of Amelie's friends and their families. I was impressed at his friendly manner and how everyone seemed to soak up that smile and answer all his questions.

Eventually, he moved to an isolated spot to gaze at the door, while I chatted to some of my friends.

When Amelie emerged, she ran up to her uncle, thrust her backpack into my hands, and excitedly talked about what she had done in class. Rahul knelt down as she babbled, and my heart filled at the joy on her face as she recounted a fresh dance movement they were learning. My feelings for Amelie had magnified, perhaps because I identified with her losing her mother. She reminded me of how I'd felt growing up.

When Rahul suggested ice cream, Amelie clapped her palms, then stopped, her eyelashes fluttering. "Can Ema come too, *Tonton*?"

I held his gaze, and he nodded.

"Yes, of course, I'm coming, jinki dikri," I said. "I wouldn't miss ice cream."

A shadow crossed Rahul's face when he heard me use the Gujarati word for 'tiny daughter.'

I've overstepped the boundary. I admonished myself quietly as we walked towards the car. "Stupid girl. Only use the pet name in private."

"So… if you're Hema's dikri, what about me? *Ma pitchounette*," Rahul chided good-heartedly.

"You are my favourite," Amelie said. "You are *Mémé*'s son, and you're my family."

His husky chuckle filled my ears.

* * *

WHILE AMELIE AND I were in the bathroom, washing our hands to prepare for our ice cream, she cupped her hand and whispered in my ear.

"Can I tell you a secret, Ema?"

I nodded.

"I saw *Maman* this morning."

I stopped wiping my hands. "Did you dream about her, darling?"

She shook her head. "No, no." Tears moistened her eyes. "She was at the gate to the dance school. Céleste told me to watch out for her. She said she's going to come to fetch me soon."

"But… but it can't be your *maman*, Amelie, she's…" I stopped.

Tears streamed down her cheeks and her face scrunched up.

I pulled her in for a hug and wiped her eyes with a tissue. "Was it nice seeing her again?"

Amelie nodded, and I changed the subject. "Do you know, when I was a little girl, my uncle used to take my cousins and me to the ice cream parlour, but we didn't have as much choice as here."

"Ooh, ooh, I forgot you lived with your uncle and aunt. Did they care for you like my *Mémé* and *Tonton*?"

"Your *Mémé* and *Tonton* love you so much, jinki dikri," I replied as I thought about how Kalpesh Mama certainly loved me. Chanda Mami, though – she could only love one person wholeheartedly, and Dennis had claimed that role long ago.

TEN

I WAS PULLING my courgette handvo out of the oven; Rahul and Gayatri were laying the table on the veranda. I bustled around the kitchen, trying to pretend I wasn't eavesdropping through the open window.

"Are you going to tell me who it is?" There was a lengthy pause before Gayatri continued. "I don't mind you listening to the music, but it was too loud. Does she know?"

Rahul groaned. "Am I that transparent, Ma?"

"Haan, you are my dikro; the first time you played that on a loop was with Debjani."

"God." He let out a husky laugh, one that rumbled into my belly. I felt something else, too, a tightening around my chest. "She was way out of my league."

"It drove us mad, all that mooning and listening to Bollywood songs. I'd thought you would've grown out of it by now."

"Me too, Ma. Me too... sorry, I won't disturb you again. I'll listen to it on my headphones." He hummed a tune that seemed familiar to me, but I was no expert on Bollywood music. "Sorry, I know you don't like these songs."

"It's not that I don't like them, it's just…"

Gayatri snapped her mouth shut as I stepped out with the handvo. Rahul reached for his mother's hand, and her eyes held his.

Mukesh walked onto the veranda from the garden. "Why all the long faces?"

Mukesh Biswas was an old friend of the Raichuras. But they behaved like they were a family, the type of family that most East African Asians had built up – people who weren't related but who had become adopted brothers, sisters, uncles and aunts. However, Mukesh's visit was also perplexing. There were moments when he and Gayatri talked furtively. His eyes shone with love for the woman, but hers often seemed saddened by the attention.

Now, Gayatri laughed. "Rahul has fallen for someone. Do you remember the crush he had on Debjani?"

My heart grew wings and bumped against my chest, hoping Rahul, too, felt the deep waves of longing that had built up inside me. I served the handvo onto plates, unable to control my shaking hands.

When I returned to the kitchen, I snuck a glance out the window. My hope wilted as I studied Rahul's profile. "Don't be silly Hema, look at him. Why would he yearn for you?"

Mumbling to myself, I picked up the baking tin without remembering to use the mitts. A seething pain ran through my fingers and I stood at the kitchen window running cold water over my burnt fingers.

He's met someone. A scorching pain sliced through my heart, matching the sting in my fingers.

Outside, Mukesh said, "Goodness, yes. How old were you?" He sat at the table.

"Twelve."

"What was the film again?"

"Kabhi Kabhie."

"I hope it's not the same this time. My daughter was too caught up in her self-worth and was far too old for you. This time, tell the girl, don't follow her like a lost puppy dog. Tell her how you feel. You deserve some happiness."

"It's complicated." Rahul paused. "What time is your flight again?"

Gayatri sighed. "It leaves at 5.30. Will you take Amelie to art class? You haven't arranged a tennis match this afternoon?"

"No, I thought you'd want to spend more time together."

I hesitated at the sink, not wanting to intrude on a private conversation.

Rahul's head turned to the kitchen window. "Hema, do you want to pick up Amelie with me? Only if you're not doing anything?"

I replied a yes back to him without hesitation.

Frown lines appeared on his mother's forehead.

Gayatri's frown revived my hope, somewhat. *Does he feel the same as I do?* But it was wrong of me to feel this way for Rahul. He was my employer.

"One last time in his company. You must keep it professional, Hema," I told myself. I decided then to distance myself from him. To not be readily available for tennis matches or drinks on the veranda.

"More chai anyone?" I shouted through the open window. My mind was yelling that I was not the one. But my heart, my heart had developed a mind of its own, soaring up and down inside my chest.

"Yes, please, I'd love a cuppa to go with your delicious handvo," Mukesh replied. "What's wrong, Gaya?" He leant across the table and put his arms around Gayatri.

"Nothing," she said as she pulled at the paper napkin holder and blew her nose.

* * *

RAHUL KISSED AMELIE and watched as I took her into art class. She skipped towards the teacher and pulled out a drawing from her rucksack. Satisfied, I made my way back outside.

Rahul leant against the passenger door as I came back to the car to pick up my bag. "Coffee while we wait?" he asked.

I made an excuse that I had to get something from the shops. He pulled his sunglasses onto his face, and I lost his expression. I was conflicted. I wished he wasn't my employer – the knots in my stomach, the breathlessness. I was acting like a teenager with a crush. Earlier that morning, I'd woken with a dread in my chest. I hadn't remembered the dream, but I knew it had something to do with him.

I wandered in and out of the shops, unable to concentrate. The news that Rahul had fallen for someone repeatedly played in my mind. I recalled the conversation, investigated every movement and cadence in his voice.

It can't be me, can it? Was that why Gayatri had frowned at me when I'd approached the table? *Does she know?*

Maybe that was why she'd been so upset when we'd left. She and Mukesh had stayed on the veranda, heads almost touching, talking quietly. Was she telling him about my scars, about me, about the fact that I was an orphan? Was she building up courage to speak with her son about me?

"But no, she's not like that," I said under my breath at the checkout. The shop assistant paused and frowned.

***

RAHUL'S CAR ALMOST ran Sebastien over as he pulled into the car park. We had bumped into each other in town and were walking up to Amelie's school.

When Sebastien asked for a lift, Rahul stiffened, his knuckles turning white.

"Sure," he said, and turned towards the school door, his shoulders hunched towards his ears. I watched his stance soften when Amelie ran towards him.

After we dropped Sebastien off, the drive to the house was long and silent. No one spoke except Amelie, who gushed about the painting she was working on and how excited she was that we would see it soon.

As we pulled up in the drive, Amelie was eager to get out, so I lifted her out of the seat. She rushed off to the garden.

"Is he your boyfriend?" Rahul's voice was barely audible.

Surprise made me fall back in my seat. My hands tightened into fists and I pulled off my sunglasses as he opened the passenger door for me. He unshielded his eyes too; they sparkled with anger.

"I teach Seb. I keep my private and professional life separate."

With that, I leapt from the car and stomped up to my room, angry that Rahul could ask such a personal question. *He's jealous of Sebastien. He must like me, after all. Could I be the one he's pining for?*

I replayed the conversation of the morning, the words 'Rahul has fallen for someone.' It was me, after all. Why else would he have snapped at me?

The feeling of elation began to expand my soul, slowly transforming my anger.

* * *

IT WAS UNBEARABLY hot that afternoon; the oppressive heat rose, and my body burnt. But I could not bear to see Rahul. I needed to get a grip on my emotions; one minute, my heart raced that I might be the woman, another, I feared that someone else had stolen his heart.

During dinner, I hardly spoke, unable to hold on to any conversation at the table. Gayatri threw angry eyes at Rahul and watchful looks in my direction. I hid my feelings unsuccessfully. It took forever to finish our meal, Mukesh no longer present to lighten everyone's mood. I excused myself, declaring I had a headache.

Amelie's protests at bath time raised me out of my stupor.

"Céleste, may I bathe Amelie tonight?" I asked cautiously.

Céleste was very protective of her duties and had explained to me that bath time was her job, not mine. Tonight, though, she was in a pleasant mood and her thin lips widened at my question.

"*Allez–y*, she has to wash her hair today."

In the bathroom, I lifted the head shield I'd brought from the pharmacist, but Amelie only sneered. For her, hair washing was a painful experience. She hated the sting of the shampoo and having her wet, waist-length hair combed afterwards. My heart ached every time Céleste reprimanded her, saying, "*t'es plus un bébé*" – 'don't be a baby.'

"No, no, not today, Ema." Amelie pleaded with her palms pressed together. "Please, I'm sad that Mukesh *oncle* has gone, please."

I cajoled and coaxed her by splashing the bathwater and suggesting she wear the special hat. When she eventually allowed me to wet her hair, her expression brightened as she realised her face remained dry.

Gayatri and Rahul were waiting in anticipation on the landing as I opened the door. I pulled Amelie off my hip and she ran to her grandmother.

"Look, *Mémé*, my hair is combed, and my eyes—" she pulled her lower eyelid down, "see, no tears."

Rahul crouched down in front of her. "It's a miracle. How did that happen?" He searched my face, and I told them I had picked up a shield and a new hairbrush from the pharmacy.

"Thank you, dikri." Gayatri pulled me to her and kissed me on my cheek.

I excused myself and walked up to my room, my legs wobbly.

Rahul's eyes followed me, full of unmistakeable yearning.

ELEVEN

THE COOLING DRAFT of air from the fridge, a small respite from the stifling heat, drifted against my cheeks as I inspected my options for a soothing cold drink. The front door closed softly, breaking my concentration.

I stood stock-still, hoping Rahul would go to his bedroom, but a moment later, his broad outline filled the doorframe. Stark light from the open fridge threw shadows on his face as he stepped into the darkened kitchen.

I gasped. An ominous crimson stain grew on his pale T-shirt. Slamming the fridge shut, I switched on the under-cupboard light for a better look.

I wore only a vest top and knickers, but my modesty could wait; his expression was pained, his teeth just visible under his grimace. "What happened?"

"Shush, I don't want Ma to hear." He reached for the first-aid kit under the sink; I held out my hand and took it from him.

His sad eyes met mine fractionally, he took a breath and he pulled off his T-shirt, one, then the other. Rahul always wore two of everything for a top. Two T-shirts, one crew neck, the other a polo neck, two shirts, one collarless. It was a something that had fascinated me since I'd first met him on the dirt road, that ability to stay cool in two layers of clothing.

Blood trickled from between his fingers as he clutched the wound on his side. I dipped a big wad of cotton wool into the disinfected water. He winced and stretched his lips tighter as I placed it gently on the deep gash, and I soaked another ball to wipe at the minor cuts on his forearms The clump of wool was bright red, and I checked the wound just below his ribcage again, then knelt in front of him to inspect it. Blood oozed from the black slash. It looked clean and precise, not jagged-edged, but it needed stitching.

"I'll get dressed and take you to the hospital."

"No, no hospital, no doctors," he pleaded.

"But it's… it's too deep."

"Go to my study, top left hand drawer. There's a tube of superglue."

I replaced the dressing. He gripped his side. I ran upstairs, my heart thudding, making sure I made no sound on the steps.

When I came back to the kitchen, there was a mound of used, bloodied cotton wool balls on the worktop and the disinfection water needed changing.

"How do you know about superglue?" I asked as I dried the wound and spread a line on the cut, checking his expression.

A sheen of sweat filmed his body as I drew the skin together to form a bond. His eyes widened and his complexion greyed. "Please don't tell Ma, she'll only worry." Sweat beads formed above his lips.

"So, superglue?" I repeated.

"Mukesh Uncle."

I thought, *he's done this before.*

I cleaned the area as best as I could and applied a clean dressing and tape to keep it in place. The cuts on his forearms were superficial, and the blood had congealed.

He reached for a plastic carrier bag from the caddy on the door, stuffed his T-shirts and the wads of cotton wool into it, and stepped out shirtless into the garden. I tidied up in the kitchen and picked up my water.

"Stay, have a drink with me," he said as he stepped back into the kitchen.

I glanced at my legs, lifted my glass and said, "I need to cover up."

He nodded and raised a thin smile at the blood-stained waistband of his beige linen trousers. "Me too."

He let me go up first as we climbed up to our rooms. I was thankful that he had not turned on the lights; he would see my back and all its undulating rutted white tracks, though he'd thankfully miss the worst scars on my lower back.

What happened to him? Why is he afraid to tell his mother? In my room, I pulled on a pair of harem pants and a loose T-shirt over my vest and padded swiftly downstairs. Had he gone into Marseille that evening? Aix-en-Provence was too idyllic for drunken brawls. *Is he one of those men who prefers dangerous situations?*

In the living room, Rahul stood by the drinks cabinet, pouring vodka and lemonade into a glass, adding one ice cube. Even though he'd only known me for a short time, I was secretly happy that he remembered my drink preference. I didn't like icy drinks; I favoured no ice, but on sweltering days I succumbed to one cube. He picked up a handful of ice cubes for himself and poured a neat vodka. We sat opposite each other, he on the armchair, me on the sofa.

"Do you want to tell me about your wounds?" I asked after taking a sip.

His gaze clouded and his expression closed. "Do you want to tell me about yours?"

I startled, but I wasn't going to let him scare me. I needed to know if Amelie was safe. If the person who'd hurt Rahul could hurt her.

"I'll tell you how I got mine, if you tell me how you got yours," I replied, making sure I met his gaze.

He took a lengthy breath. "It got a bit out of hand." He paused. "Sometimes my friend can't cope with life." He swirled the ice in his glass and nodded to me.

I suspected he didn't trust me enough to tell me the truth, but my need to protect Amelie was greater than my need for privacy. So I took a deep breath and began to explain.

"I told you my parents died in an accident. Our car caught fire on the motorway when we were driving back home. They threw me out onto the verge. A couple stopped and put the flames on me out. My family wasn't as lucky."

I tried to be nonchalant, pretending it didn't upset me, but I felt my eyes water. *Keep the tears in check, Hema. No need to bawl your eyes out.*

"Is that why you wear full sleeves and floaty skirts and dresses all the time?"

I paused, my heart skittering. He'd noticed how I dressed. It was all the rage in summer fashion, thin chiffon dresses with thin shoulder straps. I just added the T-shirts to cover up.

"Yes. When you're reminded constantly that your scars are ugly, it makes you self-conscious." I had no memory of the day, no idea who the couple was that saved me, but my nightmares were full of taunts from men, women and children who saw my back.

"Why would anyone say that?" His eyes shone as he held my gaze.

I took a sip of my drink. His reaction to my pain made my heart lift. I couldn't bear to see him look at me like that; I had to change the subject. "How long have you helped your friend with his condition?"

"Condition?"

"Self-harm. Isn't that what he does?"

"Self-harm? Yes, I suppose that's it. It started after an unpleasant episode with drugs when we were younger. Some days are better than others. How do you know about this stuff?"

I told him of the support group I belonged to. People who had experienced trauma in their lives. People who lived with scars, some visible, some hidden. People who endured the pain of losing their loved ones. While I spoke, the ache brought tears to my eyes and I wiped them away with my fingers.

His eyes softened; his brows furrowed. "I didn't know… I'm surprised at how well adjusted and kind you are."

"Kind?"

"Yes, you're kind, and you're selfless; you never think about yourself. That's something you should be proud of. I hope your family realises what a wonderful person you are."

I couldn't look at him and stared at my tumbler. There was a protectiveness in his eyes I was not ready to see.

‹TWELVE›

A WEEK LATER, I went for a walk up to the reservoir instead of my usual morning swim. Rahul hadn't changed his usual activities, the tennis matches, the early morning swim. If Gayatri had seen his dressing, she hadn't said anything.

The sunrise was magnificent; the crimson and purple blended with the brighter oranges to welcome the day. A few artists with their easels and photographers had placed themselves in spots to watch the sunrise over Mont Sainte-Victoire.

On my walk back, a tiny woman in a long black dress with a floppy black-and-white wide-brimmed hat was coming up the track. When I greeted her, she shrank and scuttled along the trail, turning back once to look at the house. Very few people used the passage, only the residents who lived nearby: the Graux, the Duprés and the old lady who lived in the compact house at the end of the dirt road.

I turned to watch the strange, unfriendly woman go. Who could she be staying with? Neither Hélène Graux nor Odette Dupré had mentioned having guests.

At the house, it surprised me to find Gayatri stirring a pot on the stove so early. She informed me she was expecting visitors. Rahul's closest friend, Bhavin, his wife Preeti and a friend were visiting while exploring the South of France. Gayatri added that she'd invited all the neighbours for a social get-together.

This wasn't the first time she'd organised such an evening. When I'd first arrived, she'd asked our near neighbours for drinks and snacks to introduce me. But this gathering was different. The warming aroma of onions and spices filled my nostrils. I asked her if she needed my help.

"Eat your breakfast first, hot croissants today." She smiled at me. "Céleste's been to the market, and the *boulangerie*."

In my family, we usually had a cooked Indian breakfast. Chanda Mami made bhakri, thepla, puri or parotha for breakfast, hot milk or masala chai and a variety of athanu to go with the distinctive Indian flatbread. My mama hardly ate it, instead preferring porridge or Weetabix with hot milk and a banana.

Chanda Mami never made me the hot Indian breakfast. My breakfast was a small bowl of corn flakes with enough milk to make them pliable and, if I was lucky, a glass of hot milk with a half teaspoon of cocoa. My cousins, on the other hand, had a dark hot chocolate with a squirt of double cream from a can.

Not that my uncle allowed the differences. He wasn't aware of the injustices; he left for work before we sat down for breakfast. Then, on Sunday, when he was home, and we ate breakfast later, I got hot chocolate with whipped cream and hot breakfast with my favourite gaur keri nu athanu. I always looked forward to Sundays. They were the days I belonged to my family. But as the years progressed, my mami had clarified that she could not tolerate me in their house and I had kept away, finding holiday jobs, visiting only on special occasions, often making an excuse to stay away. It upset Kalpesh Mama and Mini, but we met without Chanda Mami. It was difficult to go back to a home you'd grown up in when you knew it belonged to someone who despised you.

When I had arrived in France, Gayatri had asked if I had a favourite dish, whether I liked an Indian breakfast, and I'd told her how much I loved croissants. Most of my host families had been lovely to me. I still wrote lengthy letters to them, sent birthday cards and presents to the children in my charge. I filled the lack of affection from my aunt with love from strangers.

Now Gayatri had started to treat me like her own daughter. It had been difficult at first to accept her love, to allow someone unrelated to me care so much. But she also cared for Amelie, who wasn't a blood relation, either.

While I was eating at the table, Gayatri told me that Céleste had brought back chicken from the butchers. It surprised me. All the meals we'd eaten so far had been vegetarian.

"Do you want me to prepare the chicken?" I asked, sensing her discomfort.

"Haan, do you mind? I hate to touch the stuff." She smiled.

Chanda Mami had a special kitchen built in the double garage where Kalpesh Mama cooked meat dishes for my cousins and me. She wasn't happy about the arrangement, but my mama had insisted that he would feed us meat at an early age, and it was up to us to decide whether to give it up like most Gujarati Vaishnav families. I didn't mind eating meat, but I preferred vegetarian food if I had a choice, and I rarely ate red meat. I liked processed ham, though, the salty taste and the aroma. I ate fish if I couldn't recognise it and only ate chicken if it was off the bone. Dennis would tease me continually about my fear of chicken bones, waving them at me as he chewed them until they cracked. Kalpesh Mama had taught us all to make the basics, mutton biryani, methi chicken, jinga curry and keema matter. Once I'd learned those dishes, everything else was an adaptation.

"When did you start eating meat?" Gayatri asked as I added yoghurt and spices to marinate the chicken.

I told her I couldn't remember a time when I hadn't. She asked after my family. When I mentioned the two kitchens, she nodded.

"I know I'm not a good Vaishnav, I allowed non-veg in my kitchen, but Hasmukh, Rahul's father, told me that Krishna would forgive me as I was an obedient wife. In Kampala, the men used to leave for the farm to cook and eat non-veg. When we came here, there was nowhere for the men to go." She stopped and stared out of the window for a while.

I washed my hands and picked up the peeler and began peeling the potatoes and carrots for the samosa filling.

***

THE VISITORS SCUPPERED my plan of lounging by the pool. Instead, after our morning of English writing, I asked Amelie out on a word safari into Aix. She loved our trips on the bus; I pointed, and she told me the English words for the things she saw. Her eyes widened and twinkled at the change in our day.

"Yes, please, but my legs are too tiny to walk back up from the bus stop." Her cupid lips pouted. I loved her quick mind. For a child who was barely four, she had the wit of someone a lot older.

A warm feeling lifted my heart. "Well, we must ask Céleste if she can pick us up, then."

She ran down the stairs to the kitchen. When she returned, her cheeks quivered and her brows furrowed, evidence of her disappointment.

"*Mémé* says Céleste is too busy to pick us up today. *Tonton*'s here, I can ask him," she said, and rushed towards Rahul's study. I ran after her, but it was too late; she had pushed the door open.

He was on the telephone, his face stern. His voice had the same cadence as when he'd first spoken to me. "Amelie, how many times have I told you not to disturb me when I'm on a call?"

She lowered her head and shuffled her feet.

"I'll call you back, Madeleine," he said into the receiver. After he hung up, he tapped his lap. "Come here."

I stepped into the room. "I'm sorry for the disturbance."

His brows creased, and his sultry brown eyes met mine.

"Amelie, let's go downstairs."

"My favourite *Tonton*, can you pick us up from the bus stop this afternoon?"

His face softened and he chuckled. "I'm your only *Tonton, ma pitchounette*. Sorry, I'm busy today."

She slipped off his lap, her head hanging, her shoulders slumped. She dragged her feet to my side.

"Wait, *mon cœur*, why do you want fetching from the bus stop?"

I explained that Amelie and I wanted to go on a bus for a word safari, adding that it would be easier for Gayatri and Céleste to prepare for their guests.

Rahul's taut expression disappeared as he inspected the little girl, who stood with her hands behind her back. A thin smile appeared and he told us he'd pick us up at 3 p.m.

Amelie ran back to him and planted a wet kiss on his cheek. "Yippee, Ema, we go on the bus bus."

I took her hand. "We're off to Aix Aix." We both giggled at our silly little joke.

As we skipped out of the study, I sneaked a peek at Rahul; he was smiling, his head turned towards us, and my steps faltered as an image of him waiting at the bottom of the stairs flooded into my mind and something else tugged at my memory.

THIRTEEN

AFTER THE WORD safari, when we returned to the villa, Amelie ran up to three people at the table, curtsied and introduced herself. She began to ask questions about who they were and how they knew her grandmother and uncle. The two women laughed at her, then looked quizzically at Rahul when I didn't approach along with him.

I held back, reluctant. Some families preferred not to introduce the au pair to their friends unless we were expected to look after their children, too. Finally, I decided to stroll up to them, then said a cursory hello and took my student into the house. Rahul stayed behind, conversing easily with his guests.

In the kitchen, Gayatri was with Céleste, preparing chai and nasto, and she told us to join them once we had freshened up.

When Amelie and I came back down, my eyes caught sight of Kirti, Preeti's childhood friend from Kenya, as she touched Rahul's arm on the veranda. There was more to their relationship, clearly.

She was attractive, her glossy dark hair highlighted with blonde and tied in a messy knot. She had a flawless coffee-with-cream complexion, and her almond-shaped eyes were accentuated with kohl and a thin black eyeliner.

My heart squeezed; warmth pricked behind my eyes. I muttered to myself, "You're foolish, Hema, get a grip. She's much more suited to Rahul, much closer to his age."

As Amelie and I joined the guests at the poolside, the two women chattered about what they'd planned for their brief time in the South of France and tried to persuade Rahul to join them.

My chest tightened at how easily he agreed.

The women, dressed in white embroidered kaftans with immaculate make-up, spoke English with a slight accent and ignored me altogether. But Bhavin, Preeti's husband, inquired about my stay in France and my conversation classes. He had a friendly open manner and said that Rahul had told him all about me. A wide smile beamed across his face often.

Thankfully, Amelie distracted me from dwelling on it. "Ema, Ema, will you come in today?" she shouted as she jumped into the pool.

Preeti and Kirti slipped off their kaftans and climbed into the water, too. The men stayed on the lounging chairs while Gayatri informed us she was going to her room to rest.

Amelie and I played our usual game of diving for bean bags in the deep end. The women stayed at the shallow side, their heads out of the water to protect their hair and make-up. They tilted their faces, basking in the sun.

Amelie shouted for more people to join in the game, but the women ignored her. I was upset for the little girl. They must have known of the Raichuras' relationship with her.

After a lot of imploring, she threw wet bean bags at Rahul and Bhavin. They threw the bags back to her and finally relented, joining us at the deep end in our search for the bags.

***

LATER THAT EVENING, I was bringing *apéritifs* to the guests mingling on the veranda when Sebastien walked through the gate.

Our eyes met and he approached and kissed my cheeks before pulling away. "Your Indian outfit is beautiful; bright colours suit you."

His cornflower-blue eyes roamed over my kameez and churidar. I had worn a plum, long-sleeved, knee-length silk dress over a pair of tight-fitting mustard cotton trousers, the chundadi, a mustard and plum tie-dyed chiffon scarf pinned on my shoulder.

Sebastien reached for my tray and headed towards his uncle, Jean-Marie, who stood talking with his wife, Hélène Graux, and with Gayatri. Phillipe stood close by, his hand resting on Gayatri's lower back. She wore a pastel-pink chiffon saree.

I recalled the occasion Phillippe and Mukesh had met, and how they'd stood like two adversaries, checking for weakness. It seemed obvious to be that both men were in love with Gayatri. For Phillipe, it was a challenge, a quest to assert his masculinity. For Mukesh, it was a quiet wait. He loved her, and Gayatri needed time to admit that she cared for him, too.

I greeted everybody and handed out the *apéritifs* as Sebastien held the tray. We circulated through the guests and then went with our drinks to the lounger by the pool, away from the others. I was comfortable with Sebastien, we had met often as friends. He was inquisitive of Indian culture, and we fell into an easy conversation on why I wore a dress and trousers while Gayatri wore a saree.

Céleste called me into the kitchen and I picked up the serving bowls to take them to the table. Everyone served themselves from the buffet, and I helped Amelie pick food from the spread. The Duprés, Pascale and Odette, asked me to explain the ingredients in each dish.

I was comfortable with the neighbours. Both the Graux and the Duprés had young children who played with Amelie regularly and we met often at the tennis club. Rahul and Bhavin had arranged the outdoor seating on a long table, the dining table added as an extension to the one on the veranda. Gayatri had lit candles and placed bunches of wildflowers in vases along the centre. Céleste also joined us for the meal, perched uncomfortably at the table.

The evening was balmy, and the scent of the oleander and lavender permeated the garden. A melancholic ache gnawed at my heart. A stifling bleakness had engulfed me since Kirti Sheth had arrived. She had been by Rahul's side throughout the evening. Gently touching him on his shoulder as he talked, slipping her hand into the crook of his arm, filling his wineglass for him. She had changed into a pale-blue silk slip dress that enhanced her breasts;

rows of twisted rice pearls hung to her navel. Her long hair was styled in soft curls.

I sat with Amelie diagonally from them; Rahul's head touched Kirti's as he leant in to say something. She picked up his empty plate and refilled it; he smiled at the gesture.

To my left, Sebastien spoke of his girlfriend and how much he missed her. I tried to comfort him. But all I wanted to do was explore my feelings, the despondency, the ache that had built up in my heart as the evening progressed.

"Are you and Rahul putting your names down for the mixed-double tournament?" Hélène asked me.

I caught Rahul's eye.

"Yes, we will beat you two this year," Rahul chuckled. "The reign of the Graux is finally ending."

Preeti interjected. "Why would you play with a kamwari, Rahul? Couldn't you find someone else at the club?"

Hélène looked inquisitively at me and I dropped my eyes to my lap, unable to recover from the slap the word 'kamwari' had delivered.

Gayatri turned her sharp stare towards the woman. "Hema is a member of our family, as is Céleste, Preeti."

Preeti tried to justify her remark. "So sorry, Masi, didn't mean to offend, but you employ her to look after Amelie. We have to set some boundaries."

"Preeti is so old-fashioned, Masi," her husband intervened. "Please don't take it to heart."

"I can be your partner, Rahul," Kirti added.

"Don't be silly," Bhavin replied. "Rahul wants to beat J.M. Can you even play tennis, Kirti?"

"I play badminton. It can't be any different."

Sebastien had taken my hand and was displaying it to all at the table, his eyes narrow, his jaw clenched.

Rahul put an end to the debate by pushing back his chair and holding out his hand to me. "Hema is my mixed-double partner, and no one will replace her. Would you walk with me?"

We walked out of the gate, up the path to the reservoir. The moonlight shone through the trees; an occasional pair of eyes skittered away as our feet rustled the leaves on the ground.

My eyes watered. He'd delivered a verbal blow to Kirti, someone he had a relationship with, and I knew she wouldn't have behaved that way if she didn't know him intimately. Still, despite the fact that he'd defended me, the same feelings of inadequacy that had made me take his proffered hand lingered. The guests would all think that there was more to our relationship. The master and his employee. I blinked back the tears.

"Ignore them. They're spoiled rich girls who have never lifted a finger. They're babied brats. I'm not like them. I don't think of you as an employee. You... you're much more than that."

The tears pooled and tipped over my eyelids. I swept them away, angry that I had overstepped the line between employer and employee and earned a public shaming in the process. *I should never have agreed to play tennis with Rahul.*

"Tell me what you're feeling."

"I'm sorry. Preeti's right; there has to be boundaries. You forget you employ me. Once the tennis tournament's over, I won't be coming to the club with you. I've blurred the line between my private and professional life."

In silence, we walked up to a clearing and turned back towards the house, where he stopped and took me by the arms, turning me towards him. His eyes scrutinised my face in the moonlit night.

"You're right, we've smudged the lines. But I enjoy spending time with you. I'm not sure we can be an employer-employee. We're beyond that label."

My breath hitched at his words and his hands scorched my skin.

By the time we came back to the house, everybody had moved inside to sit in the lounge; Sebastien stood up to greet me.

I pulled my hand away from Rahul's arm and told Sebastien I was tired and wanted to check on Amelie, then wished the others good night. Rahul's eyes met mine and I looked away, my feelings too close to the surface and easily decipherable.

Upstairs, I fell on the bed and cried.

A servant. That's what Preeti had meant, that I was someone paid to provide a service. And she was right. My responsibility was to look after Amelie, not to fall in love with her guardian.

It was a stupid thing to have done, to find myself drawn to someone who was my employer. But the moment I'd met Rahul that night when he'd nearly run me over, something had stirred in me. A feeling that engulfed me, stabbed me, hollowed me out with pain. And now my heart ached even worse when I recalled the intimate touches Kirti Sheth had delivered at the gathering.

FOURTEEN

OVER THE NEXT few days, the word kamwari kept surfacing in my mind. I intentionally became less of a family member and behaved more like an employee in front of the guests.

Rahul had gone to the coast with his friends, and Bhavin and Preeti's mothers joined us while they were gone. The older women were lovely and treated me fairly, never ignoring me, including me in all their activities and as a fourth in their card games.

When everyone returned from Côte D'Azur, Rahul and Kirti's relationship was not the same. Instead of the familiar touches I'd witnessed on the night of the dinner, she sat further from him. Their conversation was polite.

My heart swelled and grew at the sight of her obvious misery. Kirti and Rahul were not in a relationship, but had been introduced, and judging by the lack of affection, it hadn't worked.

Why does the sight of her discomfort make me happy? I told Rahul to keep his distance.

Kirti's face filled with scorn when Amelie announced our dance performance with Rahul to "Koi Mil Gaya" from *Kuch Kuch Hota Hai*. That only made me more uneasy with her and Preeti. My position was implied by their lack of conversation with me, and the comfortable warmth of belonging that I had felt with Gayatri and the ladies turned to a burning sore on the return of Rahul and his friends.

After lunch, Gayatri took everyone away in preparation for the grand performance. Amelie gave them time for their return.

While the group set off in their cars to explore Aix, we set up a mock stage on the grass in the garden. Amelie directed like a real stage designer, showing us drawings of the set. Rahul's husky chuckle filtered through my ears as I brought out the costumes for our dress rehearsal.

She was telling him off, one hand on her hip and the other waving a finger. "*Non*, no *Tanton*, Emma comes from the crowd."

Rahul moved the chairs further apart.

While the grandmothers had rested, Amelie and I had secretly created outfits for the show. Rahul's outfit, jeans and a T-shirt, was simple to match; we found a navy-blue tennis shirt with green sleeves for him to wear with his jeans. I brought a red T-shirt to go with Amelie's denim dungarees and found a light-blue mini dress like Tina's, though I insisted on wearing calf-length leggings and an elbow-length T-shirt underneath.

Rahul was good-humoured as we rehearsed into the afternoon. His patience impressed me. He hadn't once complained or moaned as Amelie reprimanded him for not learning his steps. Since his return from the coast, he'd recognised my newly imposed boundary, and our relationship had changed in that he only requested my company when he was with Amelie.

I had insisted we stayed professional, so why was the space between my chest aching?

* * *

WHEN THE GUESTS RETURNED, Amelie directed them from the garden gate to their seats. I waited inside the house. Music blasted through the speakers, and uncle and niece stood on the stage. The audience booed, as instructed by Amelie. I entered between the aisles of the seated area with a toy guitar slung over my shoulder.

The show was an enormous hit. Everyone joined in the dancing at the end, but instead of continuing Tina's role and dancing with Rahul while poor Anjali looked on in despair, I slipped away to help Céleste in the kitchen. As I helped with the table settings, I overheard Kirti talking with Preeti as they loitered in the garden.

"I don't know why she was Tina in that performance."

"Why?"

"That unibrow, the skin colouring, she's more like Kajol than Rani Mukerji."

"Don't be mean." Preeti let out a deep sigh. "It's not her fault Rahul was distant in Cannes."

"It is all her fault. She's been overly familiar with him," Kirti whined.

"That's silly. Rahul is a kind, sweet man. You came on too strong. I told you to take it slowly, but no, you did what you always do, get too intimate too soon."

"I disagree. Did you see the way he looked at her when she walked up to the stage? Rahul Raichura is in love with the kamwari."

My lungs stretched for air and I had to stop myself from grinning. When Céleste frowned, I concentrated on lining up the serving bowls on the dining table.

Outside, Preeti said, "Hold your tongue. Kirti, did you hear me? I've upset Gayatri Masi already."

"Stop treating me like one of your children; I won't say a thing. It's obvious he's in love. He can't keep his eyes off her."

It's because you're a spoilt rich brat, not because he is in love with me, I thought.

"How stupid are you, Kirti?" I said under my breath. But my heart grew wings and began to flutter.

I turned aside from the open double window and bumped into Rahul, his hands in his pockets, his unwavering soulful eyes holding mine.

I pulled my gaze away. My body heated. I rushed to my room, making an excuse that I needed to change out of my costume.

***

ONCE THE VISITORS HAD LEFT, everything went back to as normal as it could be, considering how I felt. My conversation classes continued to grow through word of mouth, taking up more of my spare time and providing me some respite from Rahul's soulful gaze. We resumed playing tennis on Wednesday afternoons at the club. I took Amelie out on word safaris. Rahul and I only spoke about Amelie's progress and our position on the leader board for the mixed-doubles at the tennis club. Our conversation was no longer filled with topics that interested us, that we'd wanted to share with each other.

Amelie mentioned her mother increasingly, insisting that she had seen her at various locations. She became clingier with me, asking me to stay with her most of the day. Amelie's insecurities and the continual mentions of her mother took away the lightness and ease of my earlier days in France.

A few days into the week, Gayatri's sudden departure threw my role and its demarcation aside. I'd asked for clarification on how long she'd be away so I could help ease Amelie's uncertainties, but the Raichuras pulled down their veil of privacy. My only instruction was to take over most of the duties that Gayatri had done, helping Céleste with the menu selection, arranging Amelie's play dates. Then Céleste got a phone call and had to leave Aix, too.

Rahul's life and mine became more entwined, and I took over all of Amelie's care. We woke early, ate breakfast together and discussed our day. I imagined life with Rahul and Amelie, the three of us, and my sleep became disturbed by dreams of losing them both.

The crush I had on Rahul became a full-blown love affair, on my part. Rahul hadn't indicated that we had a future; his dealings with me were always courteous and distant. Still, I couldn't help but remember the words Kirti had said. They wormed into my ears time and time again.

It's obvious he's in love, he can't keep his eyes off her.

FIFTEEN

AMELIE WAS SITTING cross-legged, head bowed, in front of the family shrine in the small room.

"Amelie… what are you doing?"

"I'm praying to Krishna." She turned to the marble statue of Krishna, her palms held together. I quizzed her about why.

"*Mémé* said that if I missed *Maman*, I should sing a bhajan and Krishna will tell her." Her face scrunched up and she gulped. "But I can't think of one. What do I do now, Ema?"

I sat crossed-legged and sang one of my favourite bhajan. "Yashomati mayan se, bhole nanda lala."

"Ooh… I know this one." She accompanied me, slowly clapping the rhythm. Her voice was as clear as a nightingale, and my heart calmed.

She closed her eyes and I did the same. I recalled yet another hospital stay from my childhood and my uncle singing a lullaby. I made a note to ask Céleste if I could sing it to Amelie before bedtime.

Rahul's deep breath filtered through to my ears and, when I opened my eyes, doleful chestnut ones stared back at me.

My stomach clenched and a pang of pain pierced my heart. What relationship did he have with Amelie's mother? Did he miss her too?

"Ma pitchounette, you sing beautifully, just like your *maman."*

At those words, my lungs deflated. *He must have been in love with Amelie's mother.* That was the reason his expression was closed off. He was holding the suffering in check.

"Tonton, Tonton, Ema knows bhajan, too." Amelie stood up and sat on his lap. She pulled at his chin. "I was sad, but I'm better now."

His brows furrowed. "Why were you sad?"

She told him she missed her mother. That she was singing the bhajan so Krishna could tell her.

His eyes smiled, but not fully, as he gazed on his niece and asked if going to the beach would make her happy. She enquired whether I could join them, too.

"Of course. Without Hema, it won't be any fun. You'll come, won't you?" He lifted his gaze.

My heart ached. All I wanted to do was go back to my room, wallow in tears at seeing the pain in Rahul's face for Amelie's mother.

"Please say yes, Ema, please." Amelie fluttered her eyelashes. Her palms pressed together.

***

THE DRIVE TO ST CROIX wasn't long, and as we approached Ensuès-la-Redonne, the traffic became denser as the cars lined up to find parking for the beach. Rahul drove past the bustling town towards a wide cove with calm waters.

I had packed a small picnic of bread, cheese, fruit, wine and bottles of water. Amelie had brought her bodyboard, bucket and spade and one of her favourite dolls. We parked up and strode onto an already-crowded shore.

Amelie and her uncle pulled off their clothes. The sun had created a golden hue on his body. The tiny wounds on his arms had healed, and the scar on his side was now an angry line.

I tore my eyes away. My mind screamed at me for depriving it of a memory to call upon later. Amelie asked me to join them, but I declined and laid on the beach instead. They jumped in the waves, her sitting on Rahul's broad, athletic shoulders.

I must have dozed off in the intense heat of the sun. I awoke to a shadow towering above me.

"Bonjour, ma belle," an unfamiliar voice said.

I lifted myself to sitting, and my visitor dropped to crouch by my side. He had the face of a Frenchman with links to Algeria, with angular jaws and prominent cheekbones. His hair was curly but cut short. His skin, the colour of burnt wheat, glistened from copious amounts of oil.

I was polite, not encouraging, but he remained next to me, leaning in a bit too close for my comfort. I rose to pull on my harem pants to cover my legs. A guttural laugh broke out of his smiling mouth.

"Puis-je vous aider?" Rahul strolled up, his voice harsh, his nostrils flaring like a raging bull's. His grip tightened around Amelie and he glared at the guy who sat partly splayed out on my beach towel. "Do you know this man?"

I shook my head, annoyed at the familiar way the stranger had taken up my space. I'd been readying myself to warn him off, too.

The man stared at Rahul. *"Pardon, monsieur, pardon."* He stood up abruptly, kicking sand over my feet.

My heart raced; Rahul pulled me up and possessively tucked me to his hip. I gulped air into my lungs as my chest thumped at the feel of his icy body against my hot one.

Amelie's eyes moistened, darting between the man and Rahul. *"Tonton, Tonton,* who is this man?" she asked, tugging at her uncle.

The Frenchman dipped his gaze and left, muttering his apology.

Rahul let out a long, heavy sigh. "No one, *ma pitchounette.* Shall we get some ice cream?"

My heart hammered at his tight hold around my waist. The scent of the sea filled my nostrils and I couldn't stop staring into his sparkling eyes. My resolve to keep my personal and private life separated was ebbing. I had developed feelings for Rahul, and it required all my willpower not to show him how I felt.

I forced myself to pull away from him. His tight hold loosened, and I pointed to the towels. I needed to quiet my heart before I did something I might regret. Every cell in my lips was yearning to kiss him.

We stepped back onto the promenade. I was glad Amelie was between us. At the very least, the distance prevented his scent from filtering into my pores, and the smell of the sea almost swept away the juniper, cedarwood and moss that clung to his shirt.

"Swing me, swing me," Amelie yelled, and we lifted and dangled her in the air.

SIXTEEN

"TATA, TATA." Amelie ran up to a woman in white linen trousers and a striped Breton T-shirt who sat at the table on the veranda.

I'd taken Gayatri's car into Aix to shop and pick up Amelie from her play date and, as usual, Amelie had run into the garden from the garage the moment we'd returned home. As Amelie shouted for her aunt, I decided this woman could only be Madeleine, Amelie's mother's closest friend. Since Rahul had arrived at the villa, there had been regular phone calls between aunt and niece.

The visitor had short auburn hair and a pair of extra-large sunglasses that covered most of her small, round face. As I caught up to Amelie, Rahul stepped out of the living room, holding a bulbous glass filled with a clear peach liquid.

The woman pushed Amelie to arm's length. *"Ma fée,* let me look at you. *Comme tu as grandie."*

I approached them carefully and met Rahul's gaze.

He nodded. "Madeleine, may I introduce Hema; she has been a godsend. Amelie is as fluent in

English as she is in French and Gujarati. All because of Hema's help."

Madeleine pulled her glasses away, her flat black eyes narrowing.

I spoke in French, knowing she expected it of me. "I've heard so much about you from Amelie."

She sniffed. "You speak like a Frenchman. How long have you lived in France?"

Rahul chuckled. "Just over a year, if you count Hema's placement year."

My tummy tightened as his twinkling eyes rested on me. Madeleine's head followed his stare.

Amelie ran into the house and came back in her swimming costume. I had promised she could have a swim before dinner. "Ema, watch me dive in."

I excused myself from the two friends, but Rahul brought my usual apéritif of vodka and tonic with lemon and one ice cube. Madeleine's lips thinned as he sat on the lounger with his hip touching my thigh.

He lifted his sunglasses onto his head and gazed into my eyes. My throat constricted.

"I hope you don't mind," he said. "Can you watch Amelie for me tonight? I want to take Madeleine out for dinner."

I was surprised that he'd said that. *Watch over Amelie.*

I'd thought I would make dinner and we'd all eat together. Had he called her over to stay? Was Madeleine his girlfriend? Was that why his introduction to Kirti hadn't worked?

Though I had seen the possessiveness and anger in his eyes at the beach, how could I compete with this sophisticated, successful woman, another attractive woman near his age? Besides, I'd got myself wrapped up in the illusion of happy families.

How could a man like Rahul find me attractive, after he'd seen my scars?

* * *

I HAD CLASSES IN AIX the next day and left earlier than usual to find vegetables for the Gujarati dinner I was making that evening.

Rahul had promised Madeleine the meal, so I prepared ringda nu shaak, bateta nu shaak, dall, baath and rotli. After a dinner full of quiet conversation, snippets of information on how long Madeleine and Rahul had known each other and the odd question on my future plans, Madeleine came into the kitchen as I was preparing Amelie's cocoa.

Her arms crossed as she leant against the fridge. "You do know that Rahul has a great responsibility in Paris. No matter what happens, he will need to be in France."

I shrank away, evading her glare. It was a warning to keep my distance from Rahul. But why, when they weren't involved? Madeleine had mentioned her partner often enough in our conversation. Clearly, there was something else the family was keeping from me.

I struggled to understand her meaning. I knew Rahul travelled between New York, Paris and London. I knew he was in banking. But what could be that important for him to have a greater responsibility in Paris? The way she spoke wasn't about work. It felt like he had to deal with something personal. Did

Amelie's mother come from Paris? Was that why Gayatri had rushed off? Was Rahul also supporting Amelie's mother's family?

***

I DREAMT OF SOMEONE'S WEIGHT on me, his face buried in my bosom. A sensation burned in the pit of my belly that hitched my breath. My body tangled with his, and when he lifted his face, I gasped. The intense, lustful stare of Rahul Raichura filled my vision.

I woke gasping. My fantasy world had taken hold, and no matter what I tried, my professional and private life were hurtling for a collision. But the last week with the three of us had felt so right. My dreams were full of longing for the man I shouldn't want, couldn't have.

But how can someone like Rahul look at me like that? I had caught the yearning in his eyes, the ease with which he took my hand when we walked together, but my feelings of inadequacies resurfaced. I'd lived with an aunt who had always reminded me of my appearance. The lack of perfect light skin, the perfect straight hair, the perfect vision. She'd praised perfection in others and reminded me I couldn't stand up to the ideal. That it would be difficult to find a suitable match for me. Why was I now creating this illusion, this world that wouldn't ever exist for someone like me?

I tossed and turned, my bed no longer comforting. The dawn birdsong came as a relief, and I slipped on my leggings and a long T-shirt.

The run up the path to the reservoir did nothing to clear my head. Even the tranquillity at the reservoir didn't ease my frustration. The sun felt hotter than usual. The light breeze lifted the tiny hairs on my arms and heightened every sense in my body.

When I came back, Madeleine and Rahul were preparing breakfast. Rahul tried to coax me to join them, but I declined. It was wrong of me to yearn for him the way I did. I was the au pair, and he was my boss. He would never consider me an equal. He was a friendly person, that was all it was, those acts of kindness, the smiles.

I conducted the English lesson in Amelie's room, keeping away from Madeleine's scornful expression. She had clarified that she did not approve of Rahul's familiarity with me. *Be careful. Madeleine has already told you to back off.*

Later, Madeleine took Amelie out for the day, stating she needed to spend time with her niece. Rahul and I went to the tennis club; we'd made it to the semi-final list. When we came back after another victory, they were waiting for us by the pool. Amelie ran up to us, begging to perform our dance for her aunt.

Rahul lifted her to his hip and walked up to Madeleine. "You'll love this dance, *ma pitchounette* is a wonderful dance teacher."

Madeleine's eyes drifted to Amelie's hand, which still held mine as she pulled me closer.

After the show, Madeleine asked Rahul what "Koi Mil Gaya" meant.

"I have found someone," he said, placing his hand on my lower back.

My stomach lurched. His bright, glittery eyes bored into my soul. In that insignificant gesture, I realised he had feelings for me, too.

Everything was getting too complicated, no matter how I tried to distance myself. My relationship with Rahul Raichura was unravelling. I knew in that moment that it would be hard for me to keep it professional. To keep myself from acting on my yearning to kiss his lips. I wanted to experience my fantasy kiss in reality.

***

My nights became filled with hot, writhing bodies, my nightmares replaced by dreams that left me breathless and with an ache in my belly.

My skin grew sensitive to the touch. Every time Rahul's hand or body brushed against me, the desperation to stay connected overwhelmed me.

One more match, I told myself. *One more and then it will be over.* Then I wouldn't need to be here in his sports car, inches away from him, my hand longing to touch his as he shifted gear.

On the way to the tennis club that week, I turned my body away and concentrated on the olive groves as he sped past.

At the tournament, it turned out Rahul had been right when he'd predicted we would give the Graux a run for their money. We faced them in the final; the advantage was with us, but we had been in this position before, and their partnership was ideal. J.M. had an edge with his height and strength and Hélène with her speed and tenacity.

At the end of the game, I served to Hélène and expected the return to smash back, but she misjudged it. The ball hit the net and slipped back down into their side of the court. Rahul leapt towards me and lifted me into his arms, his racket discarded. His face filled with an enormous grin.

My stomach roller-coastered and my legs numbed. The applause fell away, and all I could hear was the thud of his heart against mine. The urge to taste his lips overwhelmed me. His eyes smouldered, and when he leant in, his breath wisped against my lips.

"I knew it. I knew when you agreed to be my partner that we would win this year." His eyes locked on my lips.

I closed my eyes, ready to lean into the kiss.

But J.M. slapped Rahul's back, making him pull away. "*Bravo*, you did it, Rahul! Enjoy the glory. It will be short-lived. We will whip you next year."

I opened my eyes and saw the reluctance on Rahul's face as he put me down and pulled me to his side. His hot hand landed on my lower back.

"Oh no, you won't. We'll beat you next summer. Won't we, Hema?"

I tried to force a smile at his beaming face.

"My husband is so competitive. Well done, Hema. Rahul would not have won without you. You make a good pair; you instinctively know where the other is on the court. It is a rare thing." Hélène slipped her arm around me.

I pulled away to hug her and we watched our partners. Heaviness seeped into my heart. I would not be in Aix next summer. My life would have changed by then. The Raichuras and I would keep in touch, but I did not expect us to holiday together. This was the last doubles match I would partner with Rahul.

This feeling I had for him was going to be my undoing. "Be stronger, you can do this," I said under my breath.

Hélène's eyes filled with sympathy. She knew, had guessed how I felt. The word 'kamwari' and the snide remarks from my aunt's friends bounced in my eardrums.

Rahul ran to Madeleine and Amelie in the crowd, then scooped Amelie up and swung her around. "*Ma pitchounette,* did you see us win?"

Amelie kissed him, her eyes glittering. "*Tata* showed me the trophy. Where will we put it?" she asked, suggesting places to display it in the house.

Rahul chuckled at her suggestions. I picked up Rahul's racket and towel and hesitantly walked towards them. Madeleine teased Rahul about his need to win and congratulated him on finding a suitable partner. Her upturned mouth straightened as she kissed my cheeks. She knew, too. Madeleine knew how I felt and her grip on my arms bit into my skin.

In the evening, we went to the Graux's home to celebrate. When we came back to the villa, Rahul insisted that I stay up with him and Madeleine as he opened another bottle of champagne.

As midnight approached, I bid the friends goodnight. But sleep deserted me as the bed became my tormentor, unable to shake the longing for his touch. Reliving the way he'd looked at me after the match. I knew he'd wanted to kiss me. I'd wanted him to kiss me, too. I wished for his lips on mine, for more than a kiss. My whole body ached for his touch.

While I was trying to quiet my mind, Amelie came into my room, rubbing her eyes. Since Gayatri and Céleste had left, she had found it difficult to sleep and often had dreams of her *maman*. My worry for her grew. When I'd first met her, she seemed to have coped well with the change in the routine. Now the separation from her grandmother and her caregiver was taking its toll.

I pulled her up onto my bed and sang my favourite bhajan quietly as she drifted back to sleep. The bhajan calmed me, too. Memories of Rahul's smouldering eyes and heated touch eased, and I eventually drifted off to sleep with the little girl in my arms.

The next morning, when it was time for Madeleine to leave, Amelie rushed out with a drawing and thrust it towards her saying, "Please give this to *Maman;* tell her I love her and miss her."

Rahul's smile faltered and he ran his fingers through his hair. Madeleine shuffled from one foot to another, releasing an uneasy laugh.

I frowned. The little girl had used the present tense. *Doesn't she know of her mother's death?*

Madeleine pulled me into an embrace and whispered. "Amelie will always love her mother. She will never be replaced in her heart by anyone. Gayatri and Rahul are her family. You. You will go away. Please don't break her heart. She is a very trusting child."

Her bony fingertips dug into my shoulders before she let go.

SEVENTEEN

THE AWARD CEREMONY was quick, and for the rest of the evening, champagne flowed and dance music thumped. The open doors to the vast club room let in a light breeze.

Rahul and I were at the top table with the other semi-finalists. The DJ blasted seventies and eighties disco through the speakers, reminding me of my university dances. Everybody was dressed in dinner jackets and evening wear; I was in a navy chiffon long-sleeved, high-back dress that I had picked up in one of bargain sales in the 6th arrondissement in Paris. Rahul wore a black jacket with a Nehru collar, gold embroidery on the neck and the trousers narrow in the leg. With the promise to accompany him for tennis matches over, I sat away from Rahul. He had gripped my hand when I stood up to leave the table, his eyes imploring me to stay by his side, but I couldn't stand the touches, the light strokes on my arm and hand as he talked with the people around the table. My new resolution to keep a professional distance had to begin tonight. I was committed to keep away, but his soulful eyes followed me as I made my way to sit with Seb and his friends.

After Madeleine's departure the day before, I'd thought of her words. If both she and Hélène had noticed my feelings, I was certain Gayatri would notice, too. I loved my job and wanted to keep it. I was not that type of girl. This feeling I had for Rahul needed to end, and soon, before the line I had drawn between us blurred any further.

I took to the dance floor, urging Seb and his friends to join me, unable to sit any longer. The need to exhaust the pent-up energy that had built from Rahul's reaction to my dress, his whispers at the dinner table, the burning sensation of his touch, filled me. When the lights dimmed further, Rahul tapped Seb's shoulder.

Rahul bowed slightly and pulled me to him. His hot breath brushed against my ear, "You can't avoid me, Hema. You owe me a victor's dance at the least."

My heart jittered as I shakily rested my hand on his shoulder.

We glided gracefully on the wooden floor. My feet floated as he dipped and turned me. Our bodies melded and I absorbed the feel of his broad chest against mine. The warmth of his hands on my body. I filled my senses with the essence of Rahul and let myself yield to him. He laughed as our movements synchronised. His face glowed, and his smile hollowed my legs.

Rahul Raichura's smile was elusive. It was difficult to catch, but that week, I had observed it often. It had been there when Amelie asked us to lie in the field and smell the scent at the lavender farm. He'd sighed and pulled me and Amelie to his side and his brown eyes had told me he was content. I'd seen it at the beach when we made the sandcastle and moat that washed away. I'd basked in it when we danced for Madeleine. It had grown when Amelie fell asleep on my lap after we walked to the reservoir. The warmth of it had woken me in the morning after the night we had both woken to Amelie's screams for her mother and we'd ended up sleeping on either side of her.

One last time, I collected the memories of how he made me feel. He had seen my scars, knew that I was imperfect, yet here he was holding me like his beloved, his warm hand on my lower back, burning through the fabric of my dress. If only I had tasted his lips. I wished for his lips on mine. Just once and then I'd pull away, keep my distance. All my resolve to be not that type of girl disappeared when I was in his arms.

We came back in the early hours of the morning, neither of us wanting to end the evening. Rahul made coffee and sat next to me. I nursed my cup with both hands as the air crackled, the tension palpable between our bodies. The warmth of the cup added heat to my burning skin.

His fingers wrapped around my hand and a sharp ache ran through my arms to my chest. My stomach whirled as his glossy brown eyes darted to my lips.

I licked my lips, hoping to taste him.

He kissed me. I was not shocked, just relieved. Throughout the night, I'd wanted it; my mouth craved for him. I knew what it meant, the way his voice hit and rested in my belly.

Now my body warmed like putty. The ache in my chest amplified. I had dreamt of how his body and kiss would feel against mine, and he did not disappoint. Everything I had imagined was true. He tasted of coffee and he tasted of almonds, he even tasted of mint. How could he taste of one thing, then another, as his tongue explored my mouth?

I savoured his kiss, and he pulled away, my whole being wanted to pull him back. But he wanted to tell me things he felt, whispering words with every breath he breathed into me. His hands explored my body, finding the chiffon of my dress a barrier. The friction of the cloth added to his frustration. We kissed and separated. He kept pulling away to tell me of all the reasons why we should be together. Why we were made for each other. But as his hands roamed up my thigh, I sobered.

How can I have a relationship with Rahul?

I pushed him away and ran to my room, unable to control the sobs that surfaced at the implications of what had happened between us. I had let my feelings overcome me. I wanted to keep my job. I wanted Gayatri to respect me.

If I did what I wanted with Rahul, I would be one of the young girls who'd behaved inappropriately with their employer. Who'd betrayed their trust.

The door creaked open, and the mattress dipped. I turned my back to him and buried my face in the bedcovers, my whole body shaking from desire and dishonour.

"Please look at me?" he whispered. "Please let me explain." His arms pulled and turned me to face him. Regret misted his eyes. "I've hurt you. I'm sorry, I should have resisted you. I should have been more restrained." He fell to his knees, his warm breath touching my face. "I'm sorry, I'm so sorry. I shouldn't have kissed you; please forgive me."

I pulled myself up on the bed to create a gap. My emotions were in turmoil, the intensity of the kiss clouding my judgment. "I really love my job. I love Amelie, Rahul. We've ruined it. I'll have to go… go back home…" I wailed, unable to control the tremor in my voice. "… back to Preston."

The enormity of what had happened overwhelmed me; my body trembled from the shame. Mami would want to know why I hadn't worked my full contract, and she would come to the same conclusion she always did where I was concerned.

I cried for my stupidity at letting my crush for my employer, my boss, affect me. It would all come out. I had heard the lurid talk of the ladies who'd lunched with Mami when they'd found out about my summer jobs as an au pair. How she had laughed at their suggestions, reminding them of my baggy clothing, unruly hair, and NHS glasses.

She won't think that now. I could hear her condescending voice in my head. "How could you dishonour our name?" Staying in Europe for my placement had already changed me enough to anger her, my clothes more Bohemian than baggy and my hair styled to enhance its natural wave. My glasses replaced by contact lenses. She had implied as much when I'd visited at Diwali. Besharam, the word for shameless, pounded in my head.

Warm arms embraced me, and I yielded to the comfort of Rahul's touch; I pulled at his soft shirt and buried my head into his chest. The smell of cedarwood, juniper and moss filled my nostrils. I inhaled his scent one last time, saving the smell of him, savouring the feel of his chest against my face, the warmth of his hands as they caressed by back. Collecting memories for a time when I could recollect them without the guilt.

I pulled him closer to me, and his breath hitched. I wanted to feel his body next to mine. I wanted his lips on mine again and I pulled his face close. Our mouths collided. His lips devoured me; his tongue danced with mine. The intensity of his kiss was nothing like the kisses I'd had before. His mouth tasted divine, his fingers ran through my hair and his groans filled my mouth. Our bodies collided and I felt his harden.

But the word 'besharam' throbbed in my head and I pushed him away. His eyes sparkled with lust, his lips thinned. The heat of his body warmed me, only inches away from mine.

"We can't do this Rahul. I'll bring shame to my family. I work for you, I'm a kamwari. You heard Preeti, that's what people will say. It was a drunken kiss, that's all." The thought of leaving Amelie slammed into my chest. I loved the child like my own, and she had suffered enough. I owed her happier times.

"I don't care about gossip. We are good for each other, we belong together. You can feel it, too. Tell me you don't feel it. Deny it." He gripped my hand, his hold tightening around my fingers.

I couldn't deny it. I felt my heart fracture at the thought of never being in his arms again, never feeling his lips on mine. What had I done? I had allowed my feelings to annihilate any semblance of control and allowed him to kiss me. What would have happened if I hadn't stopped? Raw, burning tears flowed down my cheeks. He pulled me back into his arms.

"Please stop. I can't bear it. I can't see you upset." He kissed the top of my head. "You don't have to leave us. I'll go; I couldn't do this to Amelie. She loves you too much. The fault is all mine. It won't happen again." His voice filled with remorse. "I will bury my feeling for you, if that's what you want. Trust me, Hema."

I did trust him; I knew he would keep his promise. We held each other until the sounds of the dawn broke the silence; he kissed my forehead with force and left the room. His lips burnt on my forehead like a permanent burn mark that I could treasure.

***

RAHUL WAS NOT in the house when I came down for breakfast. A note told me he and Amelie would be back for dinner. The day was interminable and tiring, my conversation classes useless as tears prickled at the thought of him. At the loss of something that would have been good.

Can I forget him, can I let him go? I wanted to tell him that I loved him, loved him like no one else. That I had made a mistake and was not afraid to go back home if it meant I could be with him, feel his embrace, feel his lips again. My confused brain flipped and flopped from one scenario to the other. One moment I wanted to be with him, the next I wanted us to be apart.

When Rahul and Amelie came back, he had retreated, his eyes blank. Our conversation was short and to the point as he informed me his mother and Céleste were arriving on the evening plane. The news of their return sent a wave of relief through me. It would be easier to ignore him. The pain of those blank eyes on my face would be bearable once the women were home.

That was what my mind thought, at least. That I'd keep my distance once they were back. But my heart didn't understand. Each time Rahul ignored me, it fragmented, one piece at a time. His curt interactions chipped away at it until it couldn't hold a steady beat.

I EXCUSED MYSELF and went to my bed as soon Amelie went to sleep. She had noticed the change in my relationship with Rahul and insisted I sit until she fell asleep. He had popped his head in, his eyes shining when he heard the bhajan. But he'd remembered his promise and stepped back out, his shoulders slumped, his eyes saddened and blanked. I hated seeing them without emotions, without the twinkle that had greeted me the first time I'd met him. These dead eyes thinned my windpipe and made me gasp for air.

In the morning, I woke from the recurring nightmare again the chanting, the fists, the pain, the feeling of being an outsider. Even the heat of the shower did not take away the cold that had seeped into my soul again.

The aroma of masala chai filled my nostrils as I came down to the kitchen. Céleste was warming up the croissants, and, after exchanging news of her sick friend, I told her of my concern over Amelie's reaction to the separation from her and Gayatri. She thanked me for the update, her expression neutral. My instinct told me Céleste knew the reasons behind Gayatri's sudden departure. The uneasiness I'd felt at Amelie's mention of her mother grew like a black stain.

As I stepped towards the patio with my breakfast, I overheard Gayatri whispering to Rahul. "Does Hema know about Amelie's mother?"

I froze. *What about Amelie's mother? Was Amelie's nightmare a memory that was triggered by Gayatri's absence?* My suspicions solidified like tar; the family had withheld some vital information from me. I'd seen Gayatri's eyes darken in unguarded moments, when she watched her granddaughter babble about the times she'd spent with her mother. That deep blackness would have taken a herculean effort to hide.

"No, she doesn't, and it's good that she doesn't, either," he replied curtly.

"What's wrong?" Gayatri let out a slow sigh. "Amelie's dreams are getting worse, and eventually, Hema will find out the truth."

"You said you'd support me in whatever decision I made. I don't want to discuss this anymore." The chair scraped on the slate tiles. Rahul's steely sombre gaze explored my face. I grabbed at the patio door as my legs weakened.

"Good morning. I want to speak with you in my study after breakfast."

Destroyed by the coldness in his tone, my body froze as I remembered how his hands had sent shivers down my back, the way his tongue had explored mine. I remembered the words he had whispered in between the breaths, the yearning shiny stares that devoured my face.

My heart told me you were made for me; did I tell you? His lips had touched mine as the words danced on them. He couldn't help himself; he'd wanted to tell me of his love. He had pulled away again and again to do so. *I've always known that you were made in heaven for me. It took us too long, too long to get here.*

He'd even sang the words from "Kabhi Kabhie" with a smile on his face.

How would I find someone else to love? Someone who loved me for who I was with all my imperfections? Someone like Rahul, who had taken away all the pain of being damaged?

EIGHTEEN

THE WAIT FOR Rahul to leave was intolerable, his conversations brief and to the point, his manner aloof. When he spoke to me after breakfast, I longed for him to grab my body and pull me to him. I wanted the sparkling smile as he detailed what he'd arranged for Amelie and asked for my opinion on what was best for her.

None of that happened. I was an employee again, the words *we are beyond that label* no longer true.

Rahul had successfully upheld the barrier I'd asked him for. He hadn't offered to make the usual evening *apéritif* for me, and Gayatri looked on with concern at the change in our interaction. I spent more time with Amelie, and the little girl noticed the shift, too. Her dreams interrupted her naps, and she woke up full of anxiety, dreading the loss of the people she cared for. I tried to lighten her mood by creating jokey words in English.

The day before he was due to leave, Rahul stayed with Amelie all night, unable to leave the child who loved him. She clung to him when he left; Céleste and I tried to calm her down, but to no avail. That night, she slept with her grandmother. Guilt gnawed at me for adding to her turmoil. She'd been cheery and happy when I'd first met her, but her eyes no longer sparkled. Now they glistened as she asked for her mother. I spent all of my spare time with her, my lap her refuge as she suckled her thumb. I taught her some of my favourite nursery rhymes and promised I would take her to London Bridge once she was in England.

* * *

TWO WEEKS BEFORE the end of my contract, Gayatri asked me to join them in Richmond. She offered me a new contract to work as a nanny, to take care of Amelie back in England.

I was reluctant. The wounds in my heart had only just stopped seeping. The mere thought of seeing her son again made my heart sore.

Will I be able to endure that back in England?

"Please, Hema, it will help Amelie settle into school." Gayatri's voice choked.

My throat constricted. I hated seeing her upset, but I had plans. Plans to travel to eastern Europe, plans I did not want to abandon.

Gayatri grabbed my hand. "Amelie needs you. I promise it will only be until the end of September."

"Let me think about it." My eyes darted to her hand and my chest tightened.

I called Mini that night and told her everything. How I had fallen in love with Rahul, how it felt so natural, how we each sensed what the other wanted. About his kiss and his words, that I was made in heaven for him. I told her about my longing for him.

I asked if the heaviness in my heart would go away. I recounted the pain of my heartache as I dreamt of his kiss again and again. How my nightmares were interspersed with dreams of him and how much I missed him.

Instead of sympathising, she told me off.

"Get a grip. It was a drunken encounter. Forget it, these things happen." She advised me to take the job, telling me it would be a steady income while I searched for a permanent position in banking.

But I couldn't forget how I felt when Rahul smiled at me or touched me. I listened to Celine Dion songs late into the night. Songs of hearts sinking, the need to follow him, the love that endures.

***

GAYATRI TOLD ME RAHUl would call to finalise the contract. I had thought and thought about the dangers of bumping into him again in Richmond, but my affection for Amelie was greater. She was not coping well with the news of the move. There had been days of tantrums, days when she pushed at her grandmother, telling her she wanted her mother.

The news of the phone call filled me with dread and I paced, unable to still myself. My stomach clenched into knots and even the knots had knots as I waited for the phone to ring.

The shrill sound passed like an electric bolt through my heart. Then his voice seeped into the pit of my stomach, the way it always had. He was aloof and professional, as he had been when I'd first spoken to him.

When we neared the end of our conversation, he said, "I'm worried about you, Hema. I haven't been able to forget that night. Are you happy? Are you all right? Are you well?"

I wanted to say I hadn't slept since he left, that everything reminded me of our time together. I wanted to say that seeing him again would throw me into purgatory. I wanted him to come back to me and tell me loved me. But I replied, "I'm fine, Rahul. You promised me."

"I won't see you again, I'll…" I heard him take a deep breath. "You should know I won't be in England for the near future, and Céleste will split her time between England and France. That's why Amelie needs you. I want my… Amelie to have a happy move to England. Goodbye."

My Amelie. I'd never heard him call her that before. *Is there more to Rahul's relationship with Amelie?* Maybe he was still in love with Amelie's mother, and that was why it had been easy for him to stay away. To leave me, even when he'd said I was made in heaven for him.

* * *

Richmond, England.

AMELIE AND I were sitting at the kitchen table drinking our hot chocolate when Rahul halted at the door. "Oh, I thought everyone was asleep."

I went rigid in my chair. *What is he doing in England when he told me he was staying in France?*

Amelie squealed and ran into his arms.

He lifted her into the air and kissed her all over her face. *"Ma pitchounette,* you've grown. You are too heavy for me to lift."

Her eyebrows knotted and she tilted her head. "I'm still *petite."*

"You are that, my pari, you are that. So why are you two still up?"

She told him of the excitement of our trip to the Natural History Museum planned for the next day.

My lungs ached and my heart released a thumping beat. The rhythm that had been out of synchronisation stabilised.

Rahul pulled up the stool next to Amelie's empty one and his gaze fixed on mine. For a brief moment, his eyes held heat and yearning, but then he blinked, and they dulled.

A sharp pain stabbed at my heart. It hurt knowing that he had to do that, had to conceal his feelings. I knew I couldn't forget him, that what had happened between us could grow, if our situation had been different. But I had told him I wanted distance and he was doing just that, keeping his distance. Except he was here sitting on the stool in the kitchen.

Amelie turned on his lap and asked me, "Can we take *Tonton* with us?"

I scrutinised his face as his gaze turned to her.

A slight smile lifted the corners of his mouth. "No, no, *ma pitchounette,* my pari, I'm sure Hema has it all planned."

Her sweet little bottom lip pushed out, a pang of pain in her expression. She had missed him the most, his teasing words of endearments. She'd settled well in her new surroundings, though. She still mentioned her mother in the present tense, but I didn't correct her. Neither Gayatri nor Céleste had whenever she spoke of a future in France with her mother. *Who am I to make her believe otherwise?*

"If you're not busy, it would be lovely to have your company," I said.

The invitation come out easily, I'd seen how his love for his charge shone on his face. He'd sacrificed his relationship with her because of me. I could bury my heart for a day. I was reminded of the times I'd listened to the song he sang to her. 'Mere ghar aye ek nani pari.' The words in the song, about how happy he was to look at her a thousand times, resonated in my mind. And I couldn't help smiling at him.

His expression closed, his emotions blanked, and he apologised for turning up unannounced, then asked what time we aimed to leave.

Amelie and I continued drinking our hot chocolate as Rahul filled a tumbler of water and went back to the sitting room.

NINETEEN

WHEN WE CAME DOWN in the morning, Rahul was waiting in the kitchen, pacing with his hands behind his back. The aroma of masala chai was missing, and he informed me that his mother had left earlier for Cardiff.

"I'm sorry Hema, Ma needed my help. Let's go to a place I know to eat breakfast." He held his hand out to Amelie, and she took mine with the other.

We walked to a little French café in Golden Court; I knew of it but had not ventured in. The menu was simple classic French with some anglophile breakfast dishes. Amelie and Rahul spoke as I listened.

My heart raced and my stomach tied in knots. I wished I had not asked him to go with us. When my *croque-madame* arrived, I stared at the jaunty poached egg.

Rahul cleared his throat. "Are you okay? Do you want me to cancel?"

Amelie's head dropped, disappointment visible in her expression.

I drew a long slow breath. "No. Sorry, my mind was elsewhere."

Lines developed on his forehead and I pulled my gaze to my plate. I was the one who'd wanted this. If I wished to be part of Amelie and Gayatri's lives, I would have to deal with meeting him regularly and stop moping like a teenager.

"*Tonton,* can I have *biscotti?*"

Rahul turned to the woman behind the counter. *"Roxanne, chèri, mon petite ange voudrait un de tes beaux biscotti s'il te plait."*

"Rahul, quand est-ce que tu es revenue, tu nous as manqué." She came to the table and reprimanded the waitress. "Jenny, you should have told me Rahul was here."

They exchanged kisses, and Roxanne sat with us. I was glad of the company. It was going to be hard to avoid his sultry gaze. The ache of having him close. The weight of the pain for the lack of him in my life.

Later that day, on the train back from South Kensington, Amelie pulled herself onto my lap. The rocking motion of the carriage lulled her into a deep sleep. Rahul and I sat quietly, reflecting on the day. It had been brilliant. As if nothing had happened, the friction between us had dispersed after the initial uneasiness of breakfast. Amelie had made it seem like old times, pulling us closer. He was as attentive as he had been when we had spent the week in France, opening doors, pulling out chairs, ordering my favourite food and drink instinctively. I'd basked in his attention, my fragmented heart healing a little. I'd begun imagining a life with him and Amelie, a life I yearned for in my sleep.

At Richmond Station, Rahul lifted Amelie out of my lap as the train pulled up. When we approached the house, he stopped at the bottom of the steps.

"Thank you. Thank you for being Amelie's constant. Her move to England has been easy because of you. I don't know how I can repay you for all the extra things you've done for her. If you need me to do anything, anything, please let me know." His voice clung to my body, the words settling into my chest.

Do anything. Those words bounced in my mind.

Kiss me, make me yours, then I will be here always, I wanted to say, but instead I nodded, afraid of what might spill out of my mouth.

Once Amelie was settled in bed, I bid Rahul goodnight and soaked in the bath. There, I recalled how Rahul had taken Amelie on the tour of the dinosaurs and fossils. She was excited and astonished at the age of them. Her face lit up as he talked of his childhood, of fossil-hunting in Penarth near Cardiff. Of the summer holidays and how he and his friends would take day trips and come back with rocks and pebbles full of gastropods, in all shapes and sizes. He pointed out to Amelie the distinct gastropods, the snail shells with iridescent colours, some white and some dark with a rainbow sheen, his face animated and joyful at her curious questions.

I'd learnt of another passion of Rahul's. He collected not only art but loved fossils, too. I recalled his joyful eyes, and their sudden yearning and how they sparkled when he retold a story. My stomach fluttered even at the memories.

Later, I slept a fitful sleep, unable to process the feelings I held for Rahul. I recalled the brief glimpse of his brown eyes watching me. The way they lingered on my mouth, bringing back the sensation his lips on mine.

His weight was suffocating me, my limbs powerless to move. I woke up with the sheets tangled, my throat parched from the sensation. The water in my glass wasn't enough to soothe my throat, so I went downstairs for more.

As I passed the study, the CD player thudded the beat of the same music I often heard from his room, a collection of Bollywood songs from the seventies. On my return from the kitchen, I stopped to listen. The song "Kabhi Kabhie" was playing on a loop, the sonorous voice of Mukesh filling the air.

Ke jaise tujhko banaya...

The words meant *you were made in heaven especially for me.* Rahul had whispered the same words when we'd kissed. Now he slumped in the armchair, an empty decanter on his writing desk. I switched off the music system and shook him awake.

"Is that you, Hema?"

I smiled as he rubbed his face. "Yes, it's me, come on, let's take you to bed." I hauled him off the chair and walked him up to his room, his warm arm wrapped around my shoulder, the heat from his body raising the heat in mine.

"I missed you," he said, in his bedroom.

I thought the same. My heart had quieted with his presence. I hadn't noticed how fragile it had felt during his absence. I pulled off his shoes and helped him get into bed. He held onto my hand.

"Goodnight, Rahul." I pulled my hand away.

"Ke jaise tujko banaya gaya hai mere liye. It's true, you were made especially for me. Goodnight, my dil," he whispered as I turned off the lights and closed the door.

My heart swelled as I rested against the door. He'd called me his heart, told me I was made for him.

But I was in the same predicament as in France. I was still his employee, and he was still my boss. There was no chance of us.

What was I thinking, Rahul Raichura and me? It was an impossible pairing.

TWENTY

ON THE MORNING of my visit to Richmond for Diwali, my stomach alternated between my mouth and my feet. Mini had tried to cheer me up with her mimicking, teasing me with little snippets of a conversation we'd endured with her mother during our visit home to Preston.

I no longer lived with the Raichuras. I had left before Diwali and was settling into the life of a jobseeker with constant interviews and applications. But I still visited regularly, and Gayatri and Amelie had become an extension of my family. As a result, my family had been invited to the Diwali celebration at the Raichuras' home this year.

Rahul's words were tattooed onto my heart. *I missed you... goodnight my dil.* Dil meant heart, and I couldn't stop myself from beaming whenever I remembered that night. A fantasy world lived within me, Rahul and me, our family living happily ever after.

That evening, when Dennis introduced himself, Rahul locked eyes with me. His sullen stare made my body burn, and the intensity only increased when he placed his hand on the small of my back and pulled himself taller to tower over my cousin.

When Dennis told him who he was, Rahul's answering grin turned my legs to marshmallows. I gulped down some air.

Mini nudged me. "No wonder you're in a dither," she whispered, running her appreciative gaze all over him.

The house in Richmond was crowded with people all dressed in splendid traditional clothes: saree, jabo pyjama, kameez churidar, chaniya choli. For the rest of the gathering, there was no further opportunity for conversation between me and Rahul. He and Mukesh's son, Suresh, oversaw the fireworks display; the adults and children oohed and aahed as the sky lit up with fireworks that Amelie had proudly shown us earlier. This year, the Diwali celebrations and Guy Fawkes' night coincided, and the skies over Richmond filled with coloured flowers and the haze of gunpowder.

I searched for Rahul at the end of the evening, but he'd retired to his study. Unable to tell him of my feelings, I didn't have the courage to knock when I left.

* * *

DREAD WEIGHED HEAVY in my stomach as I approached the house. I had not seen Rahul since Diwali. The cold, damp air of the December day stung at my face and hands. I had promised Amelie to spend Christmas break with them. My relationship with the family was no longer the same as when I'd worked for them in the summer. Gayatri and Amelie were dear to me, and I had to get accustomed to meeting Rahul.

I gulped air into my lungs and pressed the doorbell. A small woman with wide hips and short, shiny black hair stood in the doorway. Hasmita Damecha, pet name Haku, had the same smile as her brother. It reached her eyes, and I felt at ease as she spread out her arms for a hug.

"You must be Hema," she said as she pulled me to her. We walked arm in arm along the corridor. "I've heard so much about you from Rahul. We will be great friends."

Rahul? Why Rahul? Shouldn't it be Gayatri or Amelie?

Unless… I couldn't let the thought into the forefront of my mind and shook it off. My short stay would be all too unbearable if I allowed my suspicions to grow.

Amelie ran up to me as soon as I entered the sitting room and I picked her up onto my hip.

"Hello, my jinki dikri. How are you?" I lifted my eyebrow. "Doing your homework?"

"It's Christmas," she said petulantly, and pointed. "Take me to the patio."

Hasmita laughed at how she clung to my neck.

"Put me down." Amelie fluttered her eyelashes at a very tall man who was stepping in from the garden. "*Oncle*, this is my best friend, Ema."

He chuckled. "*Ma chérie,* your best friend is beautiful." He took my free hand and kissed the knuckles. He spoke in French.

Rahul followed the man in, his mouth twitching into a smile.

"Hema," the man said. "Pleased to meet you finally. I'm Mital, Hasmita's other half."

My chest pounded against my rib cage, my stomach flipped and flopped. It felt like they were checking me out. *Has Rahul said something to his sister and brother-in-law? Am I ready to accept I mean more to him? Nothing is stopping me from taking this forward now, I stopped working for him in October.*

"Close the door," Hasmita shouted, and my legs finally responded as I stepped aside. The smell of tobacco wafted past as the men entered.

Gayatri came into the living room with a squirming toddler in her arms. The familiar chimes from her keyring quietened my heart. "You're here. At last, my ladli was getting upset."

The little boy slipped down and wobbled towards the men, his arms held upwards. Rahul lifted him onto his hip.

My heart raced. The proximity and smell of Rahul pushed me into turmoil. My body stopped taking any signals from my brain, and I stood rooted by the French doors. *How will I cope with the rest of my stay if I react like this?*

He turned back, his eyes fixed on mine. "This little cherub is Devan." A smile grew on his face.

I took Devan's tiny hand. The little boy smiled.

"This is Hema, Babu, can you say Hema?"

Please release me from this, my eyes beseeched him. *Say something to make this ache go away.*

Amelie pulled at me. "Come, come, let's find my cousin Maya."

"I think you must leave Maya alone for a bit, Ami, she's sulking," Hasmita yelled after us as Amelie dragged me towards the stairs.

I felt Rahul's hot stare on my back.

When we returned to the sitting room later, Hasmita and Mital asked after my job hunting, and I told them of an internship in the spring term. Rahul sat in the armchair, occupied with watching Amelie and Devan at play, his long legs stretched out in front of him. I too drifted to the children and took the empty armchair next to his. Christmas break at the house differed from living there. I was not walking on glass, too afraid that I would do or say something wrong. Rahul told me that Mukesh had proposed to his mother; I watched for any signs of disapproval when he spoke of it.

When I smiled, deep lines appeared on his forehead and his eyes shone.

"You knew?"

I nodded.

"You're very perceptive, Hema. Haku and I knew too, but I think they were worried it would upset us."

"Why is that?" I asked.

"You know what it's like, a widow and widower marrying again." He shrugged.

I knew there were people, like my mami, who disapproved. Hindu widows hardly ever remarried. Women who were widowed at a young age remarried, but for older women, it was not the norm. The community disapproved of marriage at their age, especially when it came to women.

His response to his widow mother marrying again brought hope to my heart. He didn't care about what people thought, he didn't care about my appearance or even the difference in our age.

* * *

MUKESH'S CHILDREN, Suresh, Debjani and Bhoomi, arrived with their families later in the holiday. As a celebration of their father's engagement, they took over the kitchen to create a multi-course Bengali dinner. That evening, we all dressed in traditional Indian clothes. I had packed a yellow Kanjivaram silk saree of my mother's. Gayatri often entertained friends during the holidays, and I was used to wearing Indian clothes for these evenings.

The Biswas women were stunningly elegant in their cream and red-bordered silk sarees, their foreheads marked with a big red vermillion dot. They all had the round faces of Bengal, almond eyes elongated with eyeliner and a grace that only certain women possessed. Mukesh dressed in a long kurta with a cream striped lungi, as did his son and sons-in-law. The Gujarati ladies, Gayatri, Hasmita and I, wore our sarees Gujarati style and the men wore jabo and churidar; the girls wore chaniya choli, and all the boys wore jabo dhotis.

Eating a Bengali meal was a leisurely pleasure. I was presented with a selection of starters. Debjani explained how the women traditionally served the meals to the men, guests and children before they ate, but that was a tradition they had abandoned a long time ago.

Small portions of crispy bitter karela began the meal, followed by a variety of dishes served with rice.

The mains followed, while luchi, a fried wheat flatbread, accompanied the vegetable and meat dishes.

The next course was a palette cleanser, a fresh chutney with flame-roasted papad. I had never eaten Indian food this way, in different courses, like the French. As Gujaratis, we ate similar dishes, but they were all served together in a thali, everything together on one large metal plate.

Afterwards, a serving of mishti doi, a natural yoghurt sweetened with caramelised sugar, finished the main meal.

For dessert, a fresh fruit cake with cream was brought out for the engagement. Plus a tray full of Indian sweets I recognised – Gujarat had similar desserts: penda, boondi na ladwa and gulab jamboo.

It was odd to watch the adults; they joked and teased each other mercilessly. Mukesh and Gayatri smiled and laughed at their antics. I thought of my father and Kalpesh Mama and how their relationship must have been when they had come from Africa. I understood how the Raichuras' and Biswases' upbringing in Wales, where there were very few Indians, built up a family bond with strangers the same way my parents' relationships with strangers had grown in East Africa, too. Whereas my upbringing in Preston, where the number of Gujaratis had increased, was full of visits to the mandir, watching Gujarati dramas and going to the cinema to watch Bollywood films. My nuclear family and the feeling associated with it was very different and I wished I'd had the same upbring as the family I was spending Christmas with.

Gayatri and Mukesh Engagement
Bengali Feast

Appetizer
Ucche/Korola/Karela
Thinly sliced fried bitter gourd coated in gram and rice flour crisps

Starter
Neem Begun Bhaja
Aubergine and sweet curry leaves dry dish

Lau'er Shukto
A mild bottle gourd, green banana and French bean stew made with milk, ginger and mustard and poppy seed paste and tempered with fried fenugreek leaves

Tok Dal Kacha Aam
Red lentils cooked with green mango, spiced with red chili mustard oil and mustard seed temper

Kachkola Khosha Chochchori
Dry stir-fried green banana peels, carrots and fried sun-dried lentil dumplings with red and white mustard seed paste

Katla Maach Bhaja
Deep-fried freshwater Rahu in a thin batter of gram flour and ground white poppy seeds
All served with plain boiled rice

Gayatri and Mukesh Engagement
Bengali Feast

Mains
Kosha Mangsho
Slow-cooked mutton curry with a rich brown gravy

Paneer er Dalna
Freshly made Indian cheese with peas cooked in mild yoghurt and tomato sauce

Chingri Malaikari
King Prawn cooked in their shells with coconut milk, flavoured with spices

Luchi
Fried flatbread made from plain flour

Tomato, Khejur, Amsotto Chutni
Sweet and tangy chutney, made with tomato, dried dates and candied mango, raisins and cashews served with roasted papad, a thin crispy bread made from lentil flour roasted on a flame

Sweets
Mishti Doi
Natural yoghurt sweetened with caramelised sugar

Pera Shondesh
Saffron-infused freshly made paneer sweet shaped into flat rounds

Dorbesh
Fried gram flour beads soaked in sugar syrup shaped into balls

Pantua
Succulent, freshly made paneer and plain flour fried balls in a syrup, served hot

TWENTY ONE

I CREPT INTO the silent house. Usually, Mini and I spent New Year's Eve in her local pub, but this year my cousin had left on Boxing Day to fly to Kenya for her clinical placement. But at least I had spent some time with Seb, who I'd kept in touch with since his move to England. He had arrived earlier to pick me up for dinner before we went on to a nightclub. Rahul had answered the door for him and had been friendly but curt as I'd rushed out. I knew he'd be leaving shortly himself; the whole Raichura and Biswas clan had booked a table at the Italian restaurant for New Year's Eve.

When I returned from my evening with Seb, I slipped off my high heels and made my way to the kitchen. Rahul surprised me by stepping out of the study. He offered me a drink; the hour was late, very late, and I declined.

What is he doing staying up this late? He moved aside and directed me towards the seating area in the study. I held on to the door handle to steady myself.

"Sit," he instructed, his mouth a line, his eyes black and piercing.

The urge to laugh overwhelmed me as I recalled another night with my mama. Once the giggle had escaped, I could not control myself, and the laughter that was building up in my stomach tumbled out. Rahul's face darkened; I covered my mouth. His elbows rested on his lap as he flexed his entwined fingers. I was tipsy, no, I was drunk, happy drunk. Seb and I had drunk copious amounts of cocktails, egging each other to try something new.

"Are you finished?"

I nodded.

"You're late." His voice was sharp.

I glanced at the small carriage clock on the mantel. The hands on the clock face pulled into focus and my happy drunken state sobered and turned to anger. "You're joking?"

His lips thinned further.

"I don't work for you, Rahul. I'm a guest. I told your mother." I tried to keep my tone even, although I wanted to shout at him. How dare he say that, his eyes dark and angry, when he was too cowardly to tell me how he felt?

He rubbed the back of his neck. "I was worried. I'm allowed to worry about you."

He cared? He felt something for me, but did he have the same pain in the pit of his stomach as I did at his proximity? The uncontrollable yearning to kiss and go beyond?

"Why? What am I to you?" I wanted some sign, anything that told me he felt the same, but my throat constricted, and I whispered, "Please say it, please tell me."

"Tell you what?"

I held his gaze, urging him to say that he loved me, that he wanted me as much as I wanted him.

He let out a lengthy breath, sighed, and shook his head. "Is Seb your boyfriend?"

I crossed my arms and glared at him. "No, he's a friend." Why was he waiting up for me? Why the same question about Seb?

He grabbed my hands, and my body concentrated on the touch of his hands on mine. All the sensors in my body migrated there; every pore alive as the tiny ridges of my fingerprint oscillated.

He leant forward. "I don't want you to get hurt."

Anger surfaced again and I sneered. "So, you're here at four in the morning to tell me that? What if I'm already hurt? What if I tell you my heart hurts? What if I tell you I can't sleep? What are you going to do?" I held his gaze, wanting him to grab me and take me in his arms, make me his.

He raked his fingers through his hair. "What do you want me to do?"

"Tell me. Tell me how you feel. Is it the same? Do you feel the same?" I no longer worked for him, I was staying here as a friend. Besides, he'd told his sister and brother-in-law about me. What was stopping him? Why was he holding back?

"I... I'm not—" He let go of my hands and stood up. His eyes gave him away; they dulled briefly with a yearning and sadness. Then the dark shutters came down. "Sorry, it's none of my business. Glad you're home safe." He opened the door.

I couldn't sleep that night nor the following night, but instead relived the moment, examining his expression as it cycled through his emotions. Anger, concern, longing, sorrow and then, finally, the professional facade.

What had stopped him? For a brief time, I'd seen that look again, the look he'd given me when we were together in the South of France.

***

WHEN I WAS ready to go home, Rahul called me into his study again, and I thought at last he might say something. Everyone had noticed the tension between us as Rahul avoided me.

He took the children out on his own instead of accompanying me when I took them to the river. The first time, my eyes had watered from the rejection and the children had tried to cheer me up. Then, during lunch and dinner, he'd moved to the other end of the dining table. I tiptoed around every conversation, unable to say or do the right thing with him. He interrupted my conversations. His family threw sympathetic glances at me.

The strain between us reminded me too much of being at home in Preston. I made an excuse to leave earlier than planned and told Gayatri. She apologised for her son's behaviour and understood my need to escape.

The mahogany desk sprawled in front of me as he shuffled some papers and slipped them into a folder.

"How are you doing with your job search?"

Every cell in my body turned to ice. *Why the concern suddenly?* "Like I told your mother, I have an application that needs to be in soon." My nails cut into my palm. I couldn't look at him, unable to shield the anger that had built up from his treatment of me.

"Have you thought about teaching?" He told me of a private language school.

I explained to him that teaching wasn't an option; the pay wasn't enough for me to stay in London, even after the extra weighting allowance. As I spoke, my answers became shorter and more curt. *Why is he asking me this now?*

"But your mama's a plastic surgeon; he's not poor."

In all the time we'd known each other, I had always changed the subject of my upbringing. But that day I told him the truth. I wasn't sure if it was the anger, frustration at his childish behaviour or the lack of sleep. I told him how my aunt had always spoken of the burden of feeding another mouth. The time I'd spent locked up in the cupboard. How I could count the number of nights I'd spent in Preston after leaving for university on my fingers. How I was grateful and obliged to my uncle for taking an orphan with a deformity into his family.

When I finished, I fixed my gaze on my hands, and Rahul moved to stand in front of me. I lifted my head, and his eyes explored my face, his brow knitted together.

All the feelings I'd had growing up resurfaced, and my words were barely a whisper. "Please hold me; I need someone to hold me."

He wrapped his warm, sturdy arms around me and stroked my back. I savoured the muscles of his broad back, the touch of his soft merino wool jumper on my cheek. My body yielded to his. I'd missed the feel of his arms.

I waited for my heart to quiet. His thudded loudly in his chest, and his hands stayed firmly in their place, but he sucked in a deep breath.

When he released me, he kissed my forehead, adding to the burning sensation from the last kiss I nurtured there.

He thrust a glass of water in my hand. His lips parted as he finally exhaled a deep, soft breath. "I'll drop you off."

I wanted him to so much, but the pain of being close to him in the car overwhelmed me and I shook my head.

"No negotiation, you're not going on the train."

As I bid everyone goodbye, he took my belongings to the car.

"Are you sure you don't want to stay?" he asked as he stepped back into the house.

I shook my head, afraid to open my mouth. I knew I would break down in front of him and beg him to kiss me, beg him to take me in his arms, beg him to stay with me, beg him to have me with all my faults.

"Okay. Say goodbye, everyone," he shouted.

The children scrambled to hug me. Maya, Hasmita's daughter, asked if I would write to her and I reassured her I would.

***

AS RAHUL WAS leaving, after he dropped me back home, he pulled me to him, his heart next to mine, our beats synchronised. His hand stroked my cheek before he shook his head and pulled away, reluctance in his eyes.

What had brought on that hesitation? Was it my disfigurement? Probably. He was beautiful. Why would he want the burden of being with me and my puckered back, my missing earlobe, my scarred arm? The nightmares that had come with life after my injury?

"I'll line up interviews for you. Give me a few days."

I waited at the top of the stairs, urging him to glance back at me. *Please look up. Show me you love me.*

He turned his head and held my gaze.

My stomach fell to my feet and my lungs expanded. He loved me. I could see it in his face. *But what is holding him back?*

TWENTY TWO

RAHUL WAS AT the French doors, his eyes fixed on mine.

My stomach caught in my throat; my lungs ached for air. Then, as suddenly as his eyes had twinkled, they turned to obsidian and the shutters closed. He turned on his heel and walked back into the garden.

Earlier in the day, Amelie had dragged me to her room to talk. We'd spoken of her new friends and the ballet class she had joined.

I missed Amelie. I loved her like my own child. My heart had pulled into two as she clung to me the day I moved out. I had promised her I would come to visit often, and I had done, usually during the day, only staying until early tea and leaving before Rahul came back from work.

What was he doing at the house now, and why hadn't Gayatri told me he was home? Usually when I called to arrange a time, she always mentioned where he was, to reassure me.

I had given him a polite, professional greeting, my heart jumping and thumping against my chest when he walked back from the garden. The contents of my stomach lifted into my windpipe at the sight of him: in the corridor, on the stairs, closing the door. It was all too much to bear.

But for the rest of the evening, he barely acknowledged me. No polite conversation at the dinner table, and when I stepped into a room, he stepped out.

Later, as I was reading myself to leave, we bumped into each other in the hallway. He stopped inches away, his gaze drifting to my lips. He shuddered so briefly that I almost missed it.

I felt the memory of his lips on mine, and my tongue flicked over them.

He stepped closer and his warm breath touched my face. He bit his lower lip and said, "Hema." He inhaled my scent. "How are you?"

I fisted my hands to stop from grabbing his mouth to mine. My need to have him hold me was overwhelming. He was behaving like a teenager dodging into his ex-girlfriend. *Why is he avoiding me?*

"Is that all you want to know, Rahul?" uncontrolled anger in my voice, my rage building at his treatment of me throughout the day.

He flinched. "Why are you angry?"

"You've been avoiding me all day. What have I done?"

"I'm, sorry… it's my problem. Can we talk?" He massaged his temple, gesturing towards the study.

He pulled his armchair closer to mine, our knees almost touching. My heart thundered like a freight train on a collision course. We were alone, no one watching, no one to disturb us. He could kiss me again, and I wouldn't have the courage to resist him. I wished he would kiss me again. One more time to confirm how it felt. I had dreamt of that kiss every night. My nightmares have been replaced by dreams of Rahul, the feel of his body against mine.

He enquired after my new job. I told him I was searching for tutoring to tide me over until I started with the next graduate round. He asked if I wanted to work for him temporarily. I declined.

"Do you want me to give you a loan? You can pay it back whenever you can." He reached for me.

A current ran through me, and I gasped. He pulled me to him and kissed me, soft light kisses on my forehead, my eyes, along my jaw, and finally on my lips. He was full of tenderness, and I reciprocated. I knew in that kiss that I would never experience the same with anyone else.

He withdrew, his eyes full of sadness. "When you kiss the man you're meeting to marry, remember this kiss."

It surprised me that he knew about my meeting with Dennis's friend. I had only mentioned it to Gayatri the day before. I pulled him to me, and, at first, he resisted. Then his lips found mine again. A tingle spread from their touch.

He tried to pull away; I fisted his soft jumper and dragged his mouth to mine. He stood up, pulling me with him. Our bodies aligned; I felt a warmth in the pit of my stomach and hung onto him. He pulled away, but his hand stayed on my lower back and kept our hips together. He lifted my chin and glared at me.

"If he's better than me, if his kisses make you feel like you do now, I'll walk away. I'll forget we ever kissed." He took my hands from behind his neck and pulled them apart.

My legs gave way, and I slumped back into the chair again, my face shielded in my hands. Was that a kiss goodbye, or had he declared his feelings for me? *Should I tell him how I feel?*

The loud thud of the door pained my thundering heart. I took deep breaths to calm down. The small lamp threw dark shadows in the room and my stomach filled with fear that I had lost my only chance at happiness. That instead of just clinging to him, I should have told him I loved him. The fear turned to a burning need to tell him out loud.

As I came out of the room, he rushed past, gripping a small suitcase, his laptop bag flapping against his hip.

"Rahul," I whispered, unable to control my voice or the tears that filled my eyes.

He stopped and turned his head, his eyes saddened.

My legs weakened, and I grasped the door handle. Walk, run, do something, anything, don't let him leave.

The slam of the front door echoed through the hallway.

It was a goodbye kiss, nothing else. If he loved me like I love him, he would have turned back and taken me in his arms. He would have seen the pain.

I wiped my face and turned; Gayatri stared from the corridor. She gave me a weak, tight grimace.

Was that sympathy I saw in her eyes? Or a triumphant smile? Had she told him to end this thing between us? How could someone like me think that I had a chance of being his wife? Rahul Raichura could pick any woman he wanted, beautiful, successful, perfect. Women like Kirti and all the others I'd met at the house parties.

***

WE WERE IN Veeraswamy. Dennis had booked the table to introduce Niraj to us. The man I was to marry. Mini had already lifted her eyes in admiration at the five-foot-ten, broad-shouldered, well-dressed city banker. His square, high-cheeked face was encased in Ray-Ban Clubmasters. His polite manner had melted Mami's heart, who had declared that I was fortunate to have found someone who'd agreed to meet with me, even after being told of my scars and skin colouring.

Dennis explained what was good and what wasn't on the menu, and I heard a familiar voice approach our table. I looked up to see Rahul standing there.

My heart skittered like a rogue firework in my chest. Rahul had made it abundantly clear that he felt nothing for me, so what was he doing?

"Hello Hema. Are you out celebrating?" There was nothing in his tone to reflect that he'd run away, left me shattered in the hallway. It was back to how he'd talked to me before, professional, distant. I couldn't meet his gaze and held my hands tightly to stop them from shaking.

My throat constricted and I croaked. "Hello. Kalpesh Mama, Chanda Mami, may I introduce Rahul

Raichura, Amelie's uncle." Although Mini and Dennis had met him at Diwali, it was the first time for my uncle and aunt.

My mama stood up and shook hands with Rahul, who greeted everyone with a nod.

I found the courage to look at him. Wasn't he supposed to be in New York? When had he come back? When my uncle introduced Niraj, Rahul's jaw clenched briefly, and he turned to my mami as she asked him a question.

"Tame kaya gham na cho?"

Lines appeared on Rahul's forehead. "Rajkot."

Her thin lips lifted; he was from the same town as she was, a fellow Rajkotya. She no doubt thought he had the same values as her. But he didn't.

He had kissed me twice. It was not enough, and I wanted more. More of Rahul. The thought of his kisses made my stomach lurch. My throat narrowed, and I couldn't swallow. My senses amplified since he had approached our table.

It had been three weeks, two days, and nine hours since the last kiss. I had been counting every minute, every second to see him again. To be alone in a room with him, to kiss him again. Every week when I'd gone to meet with Amelie, I'd hoped to see him, tell him how I felt. To tell him that if he loved me back, I wouldn't meet anyone. I would tell my family to stop this charade.

"Rahul Bhai," Chanda Mami continued, "we are indebted to you. I want to say how very grateful we are to you. Grateful you found Hema a job. It has been a great worry for us that she would be a burden on Meena."

The fixed smile on Rahul's face thinned, and he leant forward, his face close to Chanda Mami's. "Hema has the most unusual gift of understanding and picking up languages. I only arranged an interview opportunity. If she were my niece, I would sing her praises from the rooftops. She is a dear... friend. I can't do enough for her happiness. Good evening, my friends are waiting."

He brushed his lips on the back of my knuckles. My cheeks reddened at the gesture. I glanced surreptitiously towards my aunt and uncle; her face turned to stone, and his expression turned quizzical.

"Vichitra manus," she said, turning to her husband. "I am so glad Hema doesn't live in the house with them. Better to be a burden on Meena than live with the likes of him."

Dennis whispered to Mini, "I think H.P. has an admirer."

Niraj's affable smile straightened.

My heart thundered in my chest. Rahul did have feelings for me? The sultry look of longing in his eyes as his gaze met mine told me that he cared, enough to throw daggers at Niraj.

***

LATER THAT NIGHT, Mini brought up that word again. "Did you see the expression in his eyes, Hems? What did Mummy say?"

"Vichitra manus," I said as we lay on my bed.

Mini hadn't stopped talking about Niraj and how well he covered up his deafness. How charming he was, how bright he was. I thought her mother had worked her charm on her, filling her in on all the details, knowing that I valued Mini's opinion the most.

But my mind couldn't focus on Niraj. I couldn't get rid of the burning sensation of Rahul's lips on my knuckles and the stare he'd delivered.

"What's the word in French? *Un homme bizarre.*" She laughed. "And how do you say it in German?" She was raised on one elbow, grinning at me.

"Komischer mann."

"Spanish?"

"*Hombre extraño*," I replied, enjoying the teasing.

"Italian?"

"*Uoma strano.*" Laughter caught at my throat.

"P… Portuguese?" Her shoulders shook as she thought of other languages I spoke.

"*Homem*," I said in between laughs, "*estranho.*"

"Polish?" She was holding back the guttural laugh that usually filled my ears.

"Stop! No more." We both clutched our stomachs, laughing uncontrollably. When I eventually calmed down, I said, "Ajeeb aadmi hey woh." I chuckled at my Urdu.

"You've got it bad, Hems. You're quoting Urdu, the language of love."

What was I going to do? One minute Rahul was hot, and the next, he was cold. One minute his soft kisses danced across my face and rested on my lips, and the next minute he avoided being in the same country as me.

Besides, I had Niraj: lovely, kind, sincere Niraj. Niraj with the golden-wheat skin, the shiny black hair, the perfect teeth. Niraj with the discreet hearing aid. I was lucky to have found someone so handsome. Someone who didn't have a limb missing or a hump. Someone who could pass as normal. I didn't look deformed when dressed, and passed as normal too. My cousin Dennis had found a suitable boy for me.

ᴄTWENTY THREEɔ

THE COFFEE SHOP in Paddington Station was bustling with people as I read my book and waited for Mini to finish her shift. My coffee had long since been consumed.

"How did you manage to get Rahul Raichura to come to the Mayfair Ball?"

My ears pricked up at the conversation behind me and I shook my head. *It can't be the same Rahul Raichura; it's not a unique name,* I told myself. Still, just the mention of his name made my heart jump to my throat. I hadn't seen him recently. Gayatri had told me he was out of the country when I'd gone to see Amelie last week.

"You know, he's adorable underneath that cold steel. It's been three months since Preeti introduced us. I think he will propose soon. I can feel it, Simi."

The woman's sharp voice sent arrows to my heart. I filled my lungs with air to calm down. Preeti, was she trying to introduce Rahul to one of her friends again?

"Don't be silly," I murmured quietly to myself. "You're seeing Niraj." If Rahul felt anything for me, he knew my home address, he knew my number. He even knew where I worked. I had to forget him, forget his lips on mine.

"What are you going to do with the child, the one he calls his niece?" the first woman enquired.

"I'm still unsure whose daughter she is. Every time I bring up the topic with his mother, she changes the subject. And he rushes off to another country."

"Do you think something tragic happened when he was in France?" the woman named Simi asked.

"Maybe. I've asked Preeti to find out more from Bhavin."

"I'm impressed, Geeta. I wouldn't want a five-year-old living with me. I know you, is there a plan?"

I leant closer to the table as the women discussed the strategy to move Rahul out of the house in Richmond, send Amelie to a boarding school and replace Céleste with an Indian housekeeper.

My heart broke at the thought of Amelie losing the only people who'd known her mother. I was in pain for the little girl who had a place in my heart. I ached for her impending separation from her adopted family, the only people she trusted and loved.

My eyes fell on my copy of *Harry Potter and the Prisoner of Azkaban*, sitting on the table. The boarding school in that book was fun, but I had read enough classic novels to know that boarding schools were also draconian.

A lump formed in my throat, but I pulled myself out of the stupor. I ran out of the coffee chain, stuffing the novel into my bag.

Rahul was getting married. I stared at the lucky woman through the coffee shop window. Her complexion was the colour of creamy coffee. Glossy auburn hair framed her heart-shaped face. A thin beak-like nose rested above her full lips.

My legs buckled, and I grabbed the back of a nearby metal chair. The lone man who sat at the outdoor table made me sit down, asking after me. I couldn't answer him and stared. My body ached that Rahul was seeing someone and liked her enough to ask her to marry him.

Why is my heart shattering into tiny pieces?

I'd spent every waking hour analysing the kiss and our meeting at Veeraswamy. I'd told myself it had been a goodbye kiss, a way to let whatever existed between us go. To move on. We had met several times since that day, and he'd been polite and professional. Not once had he shown any affection to me or referenced Niraj or what he had said that night.

I'd had no clue he had been seeing this woman for the past three months. Not once had Gayatri mentioned his new girlfriend. I was confident that she would have told me if it was serious. But Geeta was the kind of woman that would be the right fit for him, older, beautiful, successful.

"Get a grip, Hema. You can't let your feelings for him damage any hope of a relationship with Niraj."

"Pardon, did you say something?" the man who'd helped me asked.

"Sorry, just talking to myself." I tried to smile but failed miserably.

Besides, I told myself. The people Rahul associated with were out of my league. They would always see me as the hired help who overstepped the boundaries.

ʻTWENTY FOUR

I HADN'T EXPECTED to see Rahul at the British Banker's Conference, but he was leaning against the wall as I stepped out of my last session in the breakout room, his navy-blue Paul Smith suit enhancing his athletic frame, a crisp white shirt underneath, his top button undone and a red, white and blue-striped silk tie loose around his neck.

My heart pounded against my chest. Rahul's suits fitted his honed body like they were specially tailored: tight on the shoulders, snug over the chest, sculpted to his thighs. I inhaled the stale air and walked taller, anger building up at my inability to let go. To move on with my life. He had made it plain and clear that there was nothing between us. He'd had plenty of opportunities to ask if Niraj made me feel the same way he did.

What is he doing waiting for me? Isn't he with the redhead I saw him with earlier?

She'd ended the conference, introducing the speakers for the afternoon breakout sessions. Blood had rushed to my ears as Rahul had planted a kiss on her lips when she stood up to the podium to speak. For a moment, I'd lost the ability to hear.

"Hema." He reached for my hand, but I stuffed it into my jacket pocket. Lines appeared on his brow. "Why did you swap out of our session? It was ideal for your career development."

I wanted to ask why he was worried about my career. But I didn't, and I tried to squeeze past him, ignoring his deepening frown lines and the tightening in my throat.

"Can we talk?" His jaw clenched. "Did you… did you kiss him? Did you?" His grip cut into my arm.

The sudden shock I'd felt turned to anger. He had no right to ask, not after finding Geeta and kissing the redhead whose name escaped me.

My skin crawled at the man's ability to be the centre of attention. All this time, he had played me, just enough to keep me interested. He was a man who liked the attention of women. It was the chase that kept him interested. That was all this was. Once the women succumbed, he moved on. No wonder he was still a bachelor. All my preconceived ideas of who he was fell away. He preferred his lifestyle, and there I was, fantasising about his broken heart and being the right woman to mend it. Fantasising that I was the one, the one who could make him whole again.

He stepped closer, sending me farther backwards. "I know you can't forget me; I can't forget what happened, either. Please let me explain over a drink."

"You're joking." I laughed, and his eyes smarted like I had slapped him. "You're here with your English girlfriend, and you're engaged to marry Geeta. And you want to have a drink with me?"

His flint-like gaze returned. He pushed me against the wall, his furious breath on my face. "What are you talking about? Geeta! Geeta who? Why would I be engaged and have a girlfriend?" He pulled at my arm and led me to the hotel bar and pushed me to sit on a soft armchair at a small table.

"Who do you think I am? Oh…" His shoulders relaxed. "That's Gwen. You're jealous of Gwen?" His lips twitched upwards. "She's my oldest friend. Besides, she isn't into—" He glided his sultry stare all over me; my stomach clenched. "You're more her type."

He waved at the waitress and turned to me again. "Who said I was engaged?" His eyes narrowed, and tiny creases appeared at the edges.

I was upset that he had dragged me through the hotel lobby to the bar and sat me down, and I clenched my jaw. He was going to abandon Amelie, after all his fake concern for her. I realised in that moment that I would not allow him or his mother to send her to boarding school. I would do everything in my power to look after her. I told him of the conversation at the coffee shop, and my body prickled at the injustices Amelie would have to endure if he were to marry Geeta.

By the time the waitress arrived, I wiped at the tears pooling in my eyes. I had an aching heart for Amelie, the child I loved so much. Rahul ordered food, a soft drink for me and a glass of wine for himself. My jaw tightened as he told the waitress what food I liked from the menu. *What right does he have to know me so well?*

"Stop this, stop," I said. "Why now? Marry Geeta if you must, but please don't make Amelie unhappy. She deserves care and love. I'll take her, I'll look after if you can't."

His lips thinned, and he explained that he'd only met Geeta a few times. He told me he had no intention of marrying her, that she was not his type. My heart quieted as he assured me of his love for Amelie and how she was his priority. His body language revealed volumes as he spoke of the little girl.

"Good evening, sir. Waldorf salad and French fries."

Rahul pointed to me.

"Wine and Coke, a slice of lemon, no ice." The waitress placed the soft drink to my left.

"Can we have mayonnaise, please?" he said to the waitress. He gestured to me. "Eat."

I devoured the food. The sight, at lunchtime, of Rahul kissing Gwen as she stepped toward the podium had made my appetite disappear. It had taken all my strength to keep the cup of tea I had drunk earlier down.

"Better?"

I nodded.

"Tell me the truth. Do you have feelings for that… guy? The one at the restaurant?" He paused as he signed the receipt. When he looked up, deep lines appeared on his forehead. "Do you love him more than you love me?"

My body tensed and my heart thumped painfully against my chest. We had met often after the kiss. He could have said something. Instead, he was in front of me, his jaw clenched, clutching his wineglass, his stare heated. *What does he have to be angry about? If anyone needs to be furious, it should be me. I've suffered his silences.*

"Why?" I took a small steading breath, trying to keep the anger from my voice. "Why are you asking this now?"

He sipped his drink and blinked, his lips parting slightly. "I need to know. Do you love him?"

"What business is it of yours?" The words fled out of my mouth.

He slumped back, releasing a long slow sigh, turning his glass from the stem. "Does he make you happy?"

Happy? I opened my mouth to say something and then closed it. *Am I happy?* I had agreed to meet with Niraj. He was kind and attentive, he was nice. "He's nice."

"Nice? For God's sakes, you'll be spending the rest of your life with him," he harrumphed. "Nice? You deserve better than nice." He tugged at his tie to loosen it further and gripped the glass stem tighter.

"And you'd give me that?" My heart hastened to hear the words. I waited to hear him declare his love for me. When the silence grew between us, my stomach sank.

His lips thinned and he stared at his glass, unable to make eye contact. He had loved before. I'd heard him listen to the songs in his study late at night, the songs from *Kabhi Kabhie*. The words he'd whispered when we'd first kissed. *You were made in heaven, especially for me*. The words he'd repeated to me after our day at the Natural History Museum. His eyes bored into my soul, but there was a conflict. I was not good enough. He could not be with me. My age, my scars, would not fit his lifestyle.

It was an infatuation. Rahul wasn't in love with me the way I was in love with him. In that moment, the realisation hit me. I felt nothing for Niraj. I liked him, but nothing like the all-encompassing ache for the man in front of me. The man who was wrestling with his feelings, desperate to leave, unable to look me in the eye.

My heart was calmer, calmer than it had been for months. I needed to get him out of my system, to make sure that I forgot him. Eliminate him from my imaginary mind by doing what I should have done that day in Aix. Just one night. I only needed to spend one night in his arms. One night of passion to make up for the imaginary nights of passion that filled my dreams.

ꞇTWENTY FIVEꞋ

"RIGHT, LET'S GET this sorted." I hauled Rahul up out of his seat.

His eyebrows knitted together. "What are you doing, Hema?"

I took his hand and pulled him out of the bar. The heat rose as our strides matched. I took a deep breath. "Prove it to me. Do you have a room here?"

Rahul stopped and turned to face me.

"This thing. It needs to stop. We need to get this sexual tension out of our system." I swallowed the irritation bubbling up in my throat. "One night, I'm giving you one night."

He stared intently into my eyes and slowly a small smile appeared on his face. I braced myself to go through what I'd suggested, one night was all I needed. One night to obliterate Rahul Raichura from my dreams. That's what I told myself as I waited for him to understand my proposition. His face filled with a grin, and he tugged us towards the lift lobby. "Are you on the pill?"

I shook my head.

"Wait here." He walked to the toilets, and when he came back, he stroked my cheek. "Are you sure? There's no turning back if we do this."

"Why? Have you changed your mind, again?" I asked, my confidence slowing ebbing like a tide as his proximity cast doubt on my decision.

The doors to the lift opened and group of men stepped out. Rahul drew me into his side to allow them to pass. My stomach jittered. The warmth of his body next to mine sent a shiver down my spine. My fists tightened and my nails cut into my palm, but the pain helped to calm me down.

Rahul Raichura had to be erased out of my fantasy world once and for all.

"One night will never be sufficient for me," he said, pulling me into the lift.

His thumb raised my chin, and he laced his fingers between mine. His breath brushed my lips and my entire body awakened; his lips burnt as they touched mine.

The sensation of falling off a cliff filled me. I pulled at his neck while every hair on my body rose in admiration. Rose at his ability to create the sensation. I hated the feeling of losing his lips as the doors opened and we walked briskly down the corridor to his room, our hands entwined.

He stood outside the room door and smiled. His eyes lifted upwards, tiny wrinkles forming around the edges. My body basked in the light of the smile that turned to a grin again, and my stomach turned somersaults and my legs hollowed.

The room was like any other hotel room. The turn-down service had already been and tidied up.

Cushions moved off the bed, a corner of the sheet folded down, ready for sleep.

Rahul drew me down to sit next to him on the edge of the bed. "Am I your first?"

I croaked that he was not.

"Good… I was worried." His mouth met mine; it wasn't the soft, slow kisses we'd shared before. He devoured my mouth, his tongue dancing with mine, sensing me, tasting my desire. My body tingled from the touch of his hands on my back. I pulled him on top of me as I fell back on the bed and his arousal pressed against me. He started slowly and deliberately, caressing my body with his hands, then lifting away. His fingers scorched, leaving behind a burning sensation that felt like a hot poker in the places he'd touched.

He tried to pull away, but I held on to his lips.

His breath filled mine. "I've wanted this for so long; I've imagined what we'd be doing, where we would be."

He couldn't resist my lips and sighed. "I can't believe it's here." He pointed to the room. "I wanted it to be somewhere romantic, a little cottage in the Cotswolds, by the fireplace."

As he talked and we kissed, his hands tore at my clothes; he slipped off my jacket, blouse and pencil skirt with the finesse of an accomplished lover.

My mind held on to the words. He had imagined us together, as I had. Our imaginary world collided and merged. The cool blast of air on my exposed skin pulled at my consciousness and I became aware of my disfigured body. He'd see every scar, every imperfection. I couldn't let him. Very few people had seen the full extent of my injury. Every other time I'd spent with a man, I'd insisted on making love in the dark. They'd felt the texture, but I'd never allowed them to see the splintered pattern of the colours on my skin.

I removed his jacket. "Can we turn the lights out?"

"No, I want to look at you." He lifted himself off the bed and tore at his belt, unzipping his trousers, ripping at his shoelaces, toeing his shoes off. He removed my tights, stopped, and stared at my thighs. I closed them. He chuckled, loosened his tie and shirt, yanked it over his head and strode to the bedside lights, making the room even brighter.

"Don't be shy, my dil. I need to see you. Really see you." He knelt on the floor by the bed and stared intently at my left arm, then planted soft burning kisses on my puckered, deformed skin. "Blessed by fire."

His finger ran down my arm, and I groaned. He flipped me over quickly, and I felt the weight of his bottom on my legs. His tender lips ran down my back.

"Why would you want to hide this? You're beautiful. When you're my wife, you will not be wearing clothes that mask this exquisite body."

My ears pricked up. Wife. I forced the thought aside. He's saying it because he knows women crave to hear that before a night of passion.

He lifted me up, tearing at my bra, leaning over me. "Did you hear me, Hema? Will you marry me? Will you be my wife?"

"I'm only ready for a one-night stand." I reached back and pulled his head close to mine, unable to control my desire, using the ache in the pit of my stomach to drown out the ecstasy of his words. The words that I'd imagined in my fake world, the fantasy of being loved and worshipped by Rahul. I could only think of one night at a time.

He mumbled, "But it won't be a one-night stand. I was made for you and you were made for me."

My heart smiled. I was in love with Rahul Raichura. Would one night be enough for me? How would I cope if it was just this one night of passion?

His body slid down mine and his mouth meandered, leaving cold spots where he flicked his tongue out to taste me. His hands held on to my waist and he flipped me onto my back again. He smiled and buried his head between my thighs.

I gasped, my breath caught in my throat. The boys I had been with before had hastily aimed for the finish line. To reach their pleasures. But this man, this man kept pushing me to the edge as I squirmed, and he pulled back and teased me to prolong my agony.

I screamed for him to stop, to hear the tear of the foil packet. He pulled himself up onto my body and worked on my breasts, pinching my nipples with his teeth, his mouth travelling to my armpits. My whole body stiffened. Every pore tingled as the urge to release a scream overwhelmed me, and he laughed and kissed me mid-scream; my body shuddered, my limbs became boneless.

When I opened my eyes, his eyes shone, and he handed me the packet.

We danced in the act of sexual pleasure for the full night. He did not falter once. His strength and endurance exhausted me, and he left me with my bones and muscles softened from his touch.

***

THE SOUND OF a phone ringing woke me. Rahul pulled me closer and planted a kiss on my head. The words, 'my soul, blessed by fire, beautiful, cherished,' looped in my ear.

He spoke authoritatively into the telephone. "I'll call you back, give me ten minutes."

When he turned to me, the sparkle I'd seen in his eyes throughout the night had gone. "I have to make a private call."

I shielded my brow with my arm, unable to see his eyes clouded and closed again.

"Sleep, I won't be long."

The door closed and my gut clenched. Something is wrong. Whoever that was on the phone did not bring good news.

⸀TWENTY SIX⸤

MY MIND BEGAN to conjure up images of disaster and I had to call someone, anyone, to soothe my unease. I lifted myself up against the headboard and called the only person I knew who would listen, who would know what to do. As I spoke, I couldn't help but recall what Rahul had said to me the previous night, the endearments, the repeated times he'd asked me to be his wife.

Mini gasped as the thought of my predicament finally registered. "God, Hems, what are you going to do about Niraj?"

The door handle turned.

"I'll see you later, Mini."

"Is he back? I'm happy for you. Hems, are you sure you want to be with the vichitra manus?"

All I heard was Mini's husky laugh as I put the phone down.

He was a strange man; what had changed for him yesterday? What had happened to him to tell me? To finally reveal his feelings?

I swallowed the lump in my throat. I loved him; I loved him so much, and I loved Amelie. If we were married, I would be with them every day.

Then I saw his expression. My stomach tightened. His brows furrowed and his lips pursed into a thin line, the sparkling teeth that made my skin stretch and tingle no longer visible.

He pulled me to standing. I held onto the sheet to cover my body. His thumb caressed my jaw, and his sweet kiss filled with sorrow. "I love you. I won't be distant with you again." His breath against my lips. "Give me time. I want to wake up with you, all sexed up in my bed."

My body relaxed into his arms as he removed the sheet. He stepped backwards, and his stare roamed from the top of my head to the tips of my toes.

"Turned around, I want to see you. So, so beautiful." His soft breath fluttered on my neck, and I closed my eyes as the goose bumps appeared again. His arms wrapped under my breasts. "Let's get ready; I've ordered breakfast for nine-thirty."

I reached for the sheet, but he grabbed it before I could. "No, naked Hema is what I'm interested in."

I ran into the bathroom.

"And don't even think about locking the door." His husky chuckle flipped my stomach.

While I was in the shower, he walked in, his lithe body exposed. I pressed my back to the cold tiled wall, using my hands to shield me. He lathered the soap in his hands and the beam was back. "Where shall I start?"

My legs wobbled.

It was then that I noticed the tiny, raised scars on his forearms; I had helped with the wound on his stomach, but there were so many slashes all over his upper body. I used my finger to trace them one by one; he closed his eyes and sighed.

"When did you get all these scars, Rahul?"

He reluctantly met my gaze, a cloud of sadness on his face.

"I'll tell you everything, my dil. Later. Right now, let's enjoy this." He rubbed his palm over my wet body, and I was lost. He turned me around and pushed me to the wall, and his arousal pressed against my back, his fingers circling and squeezing between my thighs.

I took him in my grasp, and we both lost control at the same time, his mouth pressing onto my puckered neck.

***

HE SAT ON the bed, his back against the headboard, and asked me to join him, pointing to the gap he had created between his legs.

"Do you remember when you helped me with my wound?"

I inhaled him – cedarwood, juniper, mint and green moss. Rahul's smell reminded me of the outdoor lifestyle he embraced, and his body was sculpted like a statue, taut in all the right places, his firm thighs pressing against my hips. I leant back into his chest. The pit in my stomach tightened. Every inch of me felt his warmth. I couldn't speak.

Rahul loves me. I was incredulous that a man like him would find me attractive. Dark-skinned, unruly-haired, disabled girl. It just couldn't be possible.

"I didn't tell you the truth. She doesn't self-harm."

I sat up straighter. *She?* He'd said she. I'd assumed he'd been helping a male friend, not a woman. Who was she? Why did he need to help her? How many times had he endured her attacks? *He must love her.* I pushed the thought away. He was with me; he'd asked me to be his wife. I heard his words again, *So, so beautiful,* as his lips travelled down my puckered neck. All the feeling of belonging seeped into me. I was happy to finally see Rahul let his guard down and trust me, love me enough to tell me his secrets. To include me in all aspects of his life.

A knock on the door interrupted us. He discreetly tipped the waiter and lifted the shiny silver cloche. On the plate was a poached egg on a toasted sandwich of cheese and ham.

"A *croque-madame*," I exclaimed. How had he got the hotel to make it? It wasn't a dish that appeared regularly on breakfast menus.

He pulled the chair back for me. "One of your favourite breakfasts, my dil. Eat, I'll explain everything."

During breakfast, he talked about his excitement of telling his mother and Amelie. How he had known he loved me at our first kiss. How he dreamt of being the first to wish me good morning and the last to wish me goodnight. "We will be so happy; you are going to be so loved." He pulled my hand to his lips.

The confusion of what he was saying and the marks on his body made my insides churn. *Why is his perfect body scarred?*

All I could think of was the woman who had stabbed at Rahul, not once or twice, but many times. I tried to remember the conversation about drugs and overdoses – the struggles with alcohol. I understood. I understood it all too well. The strength needed to stay normal, if there was anything normal about a back puckered with burnt skin, a body disfigured with patches of dark and light ridges. *That's it, he's drawn to people like me.*

I concentrated on my breakfast, unable to look him in the eye. He liked freaks, he liked to help us, rescue us. I'd read somewhere that these people had also lived through a trauma, that was their purpose in life. To always help no matter what, to endure the hurt and the pain.

I folded the napkin and stood up to distance myself from him. I didn't need rescuing; I could look after myself.

He pulled me to his lap and explained how he had endured Rajni's rage many times. He told me of how they'd met when they both worked in Paris, how he had tried to help with Rajni's drug addiction. He talked of the guilt of not being able to help her. "I should have helped her more, but I couldn't." He swiped at his nose with his napkin, his eyes wet.

That's what it was, he needed to help her because he had feelings for her. She wasn't just a work friend, there was more to it. How gullible and stupid of me to think that I was the one.

"Do you... do you...?" My words halted in my throat. Could I hear him say those words about Rajni, about anyone else?

163

He lifted me to sit facing him, pushing my legs to straddle his.

"No, no, I love you. Only you." His lips met mine, and his tender kiss told me of the love he felt for me. I wanted proof of his love, and I pulled him to the bed, flung off my towelling gown.

His eyes softened and he pushed off his gown and we made love again. I savoured every touch, taste, and when Rahul pulled away, I pulled him back, unable to let go of his soft mouth that fitted so perfectly with mine. I wanted him to know that I fitted perfectly with him. That I wanted to be the only one he rescued, if that was what he needed. I needed it too.

Rahul Raichura, the enigma, had finally revealed a secret he had been holding. I knew he hadn't told me everything. There was something in his voice when he talked of Rajni's drug habit. A piece of information he was holding back, but I let myself relish the acknowledgement of his love. I let myself believe that he loved me.

TWENTY SEVEN

WE STOPPED AT Newport Pagnell service station for a comfort break, and when I came out of the toilets, Rahul was on the phone. I browsed in the shop until he finished.

"What's happened?"

The shutters fell, his eyes flattened and the mask appeared. "Nothing, nothing, do you want a drink?" He held up a can of soft drink. I declined.

The drive back to my flat was long and strained. He stared at the road, his jaw clenched. By the time we pulled up at my flat, I was battling with the build-up of misery. The silent drive had given him time to process what had happened. He'd realised I wasn't what he wanted. Too young, too ugly to be the right fit. Why had the phone calls made him close off?

"Please tell me what the call was about?"

He turned towards me. "It's too complicated. Please, Hema, I need to—" He held me to him.

My heart raced against his and I thought, *this is his last goodbye*. He wasn't seeking forever. Something or someone had reminded him we were incompatible. It was a one-night stand.

I pushed him away angrily, "You got carried away. It was… only sexual attraction, nothing more. But I was honest with you, Rahul. There wasn't any need for you to say all those things. All the lies to make me feel the way I do. You made me believe that you felt something."

I hauled my bag out of the boot. It wasn't a sexual attraction for me. I knew I loved Rahul and couldn't marry Niraj. A heaviness filled my body, and the weight of carrying the pain increased as I recalled all the words he had whispered in my ear. I wanted to remember it all. I wished I had cherished it and stored it in my memory. Just like the night of the kiss, every smell, touch, word.

He put my bag back in the boot. "Darling, look at me."

I inhaled and fisted my hands to prevent him for holding them.

"I told you one night would not be enough. It isn't. But I'm sorry, I need to sort something out." Deep furrows appeared on his forehead, as he searched my face. "You're cross. I love you. I didn't lie." He kissed my forehead. "You were made for me. I can't lose you now. Please, I just can't."

His words eased the heaviness in my tummy, and I drew his mouth to mine.

***

"ARE YOU going to tell your mother tonight?" I asked Rahul.

"Can't, she's in Cardiff. I don't want to tell her on the phone, and we'll speak to Amelie together. Are you sure you can't come stay tonight?" The glow from his smile caused me to wilt, and I kissed him again.

"I can't," I replied, reluctant to let the kiss go. "I have a ton of washing. I'll see you tomorrow for lunch, though."

I pushed him away and he walked down the stairs, turned, and lifted his head. "Lunch tomorrow, my dil."

As soon as I closed the door, Mini stepped out of the kitchen.

She thrust a glass of vodka and lemonade, no ice, at me. "Fill me in, I want all the details."

I told her everything. She listened intently, and she was flustered when I mentioned the things he had done.

"How many times did you orgasm again?"

I exhaled; my cheeks reddened.

"Does Rahul have a friend?" she asked with wide eyes.

***

"DARLING," RAHUL said on the phone later that evening, "I'm sorry I can't meet you for lunch tomorrow. I have to leave for France."

"France, why France?" I thought of Rajni. "Are you going to Aix?"

"No, Paris. I'll tell you everything when I get back. I promise, my heart; I promise. I love you. But I have to go tonight on the ten-thirty flight."

I gripped the handset until it went dead; I knew in my core he was holding onto something, a secret. Why the urgency, why tonight?

The fluttering in my stomach stilled and became heavy as a boulder.

***

RAHUL RANG ME every day after work. Our conversations were not of love and longing – of lovers wanting to extend the call, muttering terms of endearments. The calls were precise as we informed each other of how we felt and how we wanted to spend our life together.

I held in my frustration at his inability to confide in me. Part of me thought that if he loved me, he would tell me every one of his secrets. Another part of me told me to stop being clingy, that his work prevented him for telling me everything.

But I knew that this wasn't work-related; I'd heard him talk about deals and mergers before. As the days apart lengthened, the knots in my stomach strengthened.

He rang later than usual on Thursday evening, his tone lukewarm. He said all the appropriate words, but the warmth was no longer audible.

"I'm stuck here, my dil. I can't leave until Sunday."

I swallowed the disappointment down. "Don't worry, Rahul. You need to do what you need to. I'm aware of your work commitments."

I used those words to check that it was work-related, knowing that what he was about to say would not confirm it.

He sighed. The silence scratched at my heart.

"It is to do with work, this extension?" I enquired. My legs collapsed as I squatted on the floor, fearing that the answer was going to send me into a spiral of misery.

"I haven't been straightforward with you. I'm here to help Rajni."

Anger choked at my throat and I took a simmering breath. He had spoken to me daily. Not once had he mentioned Rajni. That he was helping a woman who had hurt him, someone he felt responsible for. Someone who he had rushed to help. What was she to him and why had he said she was just a friend?

"What is she doing in Paris? You are in Paris?" I kicked at the telephone stool, and it thudded onto the floor. There was a knock on the wall from the flat next door.

At Rahul's silence, I recalled the conversation with Madeleine, the warning. I demanded to know if there was more to the relationship than he had said.

The silence chipped at my heart, and he released a deep breath and replied he would explain everything on Sunday. When it was time to say goodbye, he said he loved me, but I did not repeat the words back to him. My inadequacy and frustration gnawed at my heart. *I will never be good enough. Even a woman with anger issues is better than me.*

Friday evening's phone call was short and curt. I held onto my frustration. Saturday, Rahul rang briefly to tell me of the flight time and what time he would arrive at my flat. Saturday night, my sleep was disturbed with a sense of foreboding, Rahul slipping from my arms, taken by an unknown woman with a knife to his throat.

I woke up with a start in the early hours of Sunday morning, unable to sleep, the pain and anguish in his face etched in my mind. The wait to see him again was agonising. Fire ants gnawed on my stomach walls. I watched the clock, but the hands remained static.

Mini was working, so I had no one to distract me, to keep me buoyant. She, too, had noticed the change in my mood since the phone call. I stomped about the flat, ate in silence and stayed in my room. Rahul had closed off again. He had said the right words, but they hadn't reached my chest. They'd whispered briefly against my eardrums and floated away, like an ethereal dream.

What am I going to do next? I loved Amelie; my soul ached at not seeing her again. My mind filled with the time I'd moved out and her anguished cries, and I scolded myself for jeopardising my relationship with the child I loved. I needed to continue to see her. I admonished myself for letting my feelings for Rahul ruin the one good thing that had happened as a result of my meeting him. I would need to emphasise to him that our one night of passion could not, should not, stop me from visiting.

The ringing of doorbell startled me out of my torment. Rahul rushed up the stairs and kissed me with longing until my lungs yelled for air.

All the tension of my solitary wait washed away in that embrace. *He does love me. He did miss me as much as I missed him.*

We ate our simple meal of chana nu shaak, puri, chaas and athanu. His lips curled up as he saw what I'd made. "I love how you make your chana, the sourness from the tamarind and the sweetness. How do you get it just so?" He held my hand across the table as we ate.

My stomach relaxed a little, but the rare precious grin never appeared. His lips fluttered upwards as I talked about how excited Amelie would be when we told her.

After lunch, we cuddled in the front room, neither of us wanting to talk as we watched the TV. My body felt the change before my mind registered it. Rahul's body stiffened. His arms held me tight, but they didn't embrace me, cherish me. I sensed his body shutting me out. His hand no longer caressed my arm. He reached for the remote, turned the TV off, lifted me off his chest and grasped both my hands in his.

He spoke hesitantly at first. "My love, my dil, this will not work. My world is too complicated. It was wrong of me to take advantage of you last weekend."

My body filled with sorrow and prickly tears built behind my eyes. "Please, don't do this to me; don't close yourself off. I'm sorry I was cross. Please tell me the truth."

"I'm not good enough. I can marry no one. I let the dream of another life overwhelm me. I let my jealousy get in the way of your happiness. Marry Niraj."

I pleaded between my sudden sobs. "Please— why are you saying this now? What happened? Who is Rajni? What does she mean to you?" I stood up, unable to sit.

171

Rahul looked up at me, his shoulders slumped, his hands aloft, unable to fall back down from where I'd let them go. "I'm sorry, this can't go on. I will make you miserable, and you'll hate me. I have responsibilities. I have to think of Amelie."

My knees buckled and I fell onto the floor, pleading with him, tears trailing down my face. Telling him I would never harm Amelie.

He sank on his haunches to face me, lowering his face to meet mine. Flat eyes looked back at me, his cheeks damp.

Time slowed and stretched. Trails of tears rippled down my neck. Rahul's eyes held mine, and I couldn't let them go. But they were no longer the eyes that shone and twinkled. They revealed nothing. They were empty of all emotion.

"Forget me." He stood up, his arms hanging limply by his side.

I clung to his legs; he hauled me up and I kissed his unyielding lips. I wanted him to kiss me with love, leave me one last kiss to remember him by. A kiss for him to remember me by.

He removed my hands from behind his neck. "Listen to me, Hema. This won't work, forget me. I will try to forget you. I won't stop you from seeing Amelie or Ma. I can see how much they mean to you."

I could not watch him leave and turned my back on him. He hesitated, and then I heard the door shut.

For a brief time, I had held onto the pleasure of being loved by my only love. I thought I'd loved before, but they were schoolgirl crushes. The sense of completeness, the sense of belonging that he gave me was gone. The only person I belonged to had left, and a hole began to grow in my heart.

Why would someone like Rahul Raichura make me his bride?

TWENTY EIGHT

I COULDN'T DEAL with the heartache and begged Mini to call work asking for leave. The unbearable loss of Rahul etched itself into my body and soul. I still felt his arms, his lips, at the most inappropriate times.

Mini had a trying and busy schedule at work and would leave me food in the fridge as she'd always done, hoping it would help me process my feelings. I ignored the food, unable to keep any morsel down, and she would come home and use her precious free time to cajole me to eat.

One of the things I'd learnt from group therapy was the many ways people find to destroy themselves, a little at a time. And the only control I had was to deprive myself of the thing that could sustain me and keep me healthy. I began to pretend I'd eaten the food, hiding it in the bin outside. Why should I live? Why should I endure the pain?

I heard a gentle knock and Mini entered my room and sat on the edge of the bed.

"Are you ready to tell me what happened?" Her eyes filled with concern and something else.

I told her in between sobs of Rahul's unwillingness to commit to our relationship. His words scratched my eardrums. *I let my jealousy get in the way of your happiness. Marry Niraj.*

"So, are you?" Mini's voice halted as she flashed a fleeting look of pity. "Going to marry Niraj?"

Mini never looked at me like that. I'd become such a wretch that I'd made even my sister feel sorry for me.

I couldn't answer her, and instead wallowed in self-pity. She pulled me into a hug before leaving the room, her shoulders slumped. I'd unloaded my burden onto my sister who was usually jolly and optimistic, but that day, she was worn out, wrung dry of all joy.

For days I endured her low moods, her lack of smiles. Then I thought of how I was adding to her already heavy work schedule at the hospital and decided to make changes in my life. I had to see Amelie again, I had to go back to work, but first, I had to have an important conversation.

The front door opened. I was waiting for Mini, ready to discuss what I planned to do. Her eyes widened at seeing my pencil skirt and soft silk blouse instead of the same T-shirt and harem pants I'd worn for days.

"Are you off somewhere special?"

I replied, but my answer didn't quite register. She slipped off her shoes and rubbed at her feet one at a time.

I repeated my answer again. "I'm meeting Niraj for lunch to tell him the truth about my feelings."

"Okay…" She walked into the kitchen and poured herself a glass of water from the tap at the sink, her back to me. She took a deep breath before turning around. Her lips thinned.

"I'll need your help?"

"Why?" Her tone was flat.

"'Cause we're going home." I needed her to come with me to Preston, for when I told her parents of the decision I'd made about my future.

She pulled herself straighter. "I have next weekend off. Can't you and Niraj go alone?"

I'd expected a bit more support, but Mini was too distant, too disconnected.

I pulled her down to sit at the table. "Tough shifts this week?"

She nodded. "I hate this round. So sad to see so many old people at the end of their life."

I filled a pan with water, added tea leaves, sugar and masala and waited for the tea to brew. I popped two pieces of brown bread into the toaster and made my big sister some breakfast. As I watched, she sat holding her head in hands, staring at the kitchen table, all her positive energy sapped out of her.

I'd made her like this. I'd completely forgotten about her new role in the Geriatric ward. I knew I shouldn't burden her further, that I needed to get a backbone and stand up to my uncle and aunt on my own.

Once she'd taken a few bites of the toast and sipped from her mug of tea, I reached across the table and squeezed her hand. "You don't have to come. I'll go and tell them the whole thing's off."

"What's off?"

"I'm having lunch with Niraj, what's wrong with you?"

Her eyes focused on me, and she rubbed at her forehead. "Sorry, tell me again, I'm all ears."

When I left an hour later to meet Niraj, Mini was a lot more like herself. Her eyes had regained their lustre.

***

MORGAN STANLEY in Cabot Square was minutes away from my building in Canary Wharf. Both Dennis and Niraj were based there. The building Niraj worked in was a brick lattice work with huge glass enclosed inside it. The receptionist asked for my name and rang through to Niraj to let him know I was waiting in reception.

Niraj was wearing a navy blue suit, his double cuff just visible, with a silk abstract necktie against a white shirt and a bright red polka-dot square protruding from his jacket breast pocket. As soon as his eyes found me, he quickened his pace.

I stood up as he leant in to kiss me on my lips, but I turned my head and his kiss landed on my cheek. We had met several times and we'd even kissed, but I had to let him know how I felt once and for all. It was too selfish of me to keep him in the dark, and I hadn't spoken to him in a week.

He held my hand, his eyes searching mine. "Are you feeling better?"

I told him I was okay and feigned being too hungry for conversation.

All around Cabot Square, there were cafes and restaurants for busy people to grab quick lunches and meet with the rest of their teams while keeping some semblance of a normal life. The whole of Canary Wharf was filled with people working long days and not spending enough hours at home. Most people who worked in the City had a favourite spot, and Niraj had his, a lovely Spanish tapas restaurant. He held my elbow and guided me inside.

The table was on the mezzanine and Niraj ordered a selection of tapas before we tucked into our mains of seafood paella. We ate and exchanged news on what had happened during our time apart until the coffees arrived. I was not nervous. I admired Niraj's sensitivity, he was very empathetic to people's moods. It was one of the things that made it easier for me to meet with him again.

"What's up?" he asked after taking his first sip of coffee.

I told him of my betrayal, of how I'd slept with Rahul even though we were supposed to be seeing each other. I told him how I couldn't carry on seeing him, building up a false hope that one day he and I could be a couple.

He listened as I spoke of my feelings for another man, a man who had rejected me. A man who was in love with someone else. A man who held many secrets. Niraj reached for my hand and told me he was glad I'd finally made up my mind.

"You know why I agreed to meet you and why I like you, Hema? It's because, like me, your disability doesn't define you. I don't want to be judged by these." He tapped his ear. He lifted my shirt sleeve and caressed the burn marks on my arm. "You don't allow this to define you, either."

The touch of his fingers brought tears to my eyes and a group of people walked past, looking slightly embarrassed at my sign of weakness. They must have thought I was being reprimanded for a big loss. It usually happened like that. A friend taking you out for lunch to forewarn you of your impending dismissal.

By the time I left Canary Wharf, my burden had lessened, but my stomach was like a heaving sea. The next big conversation was going to be tougher, but as I made my way to Richmond, I tried to forget the impending storm my announcement would create with my aunt and uncle.

I was aware that Rahul Raichura had taken himself to live in Paris for the foreseeable future, and my time with Gayatri and Amelie was more precious than before. How long would I keep meeting him with his family? My life was now full of hard choices.

***

AT AMELIE'S performance, she and the other girls twirled and pirouetted to "Waltz of the Flowers" from *The Nutcracker*. Their bright pink costumes mimicked flowers, their arms waving like petals blowing in the wind. I loved Tchaikovsky's ballet, the story of Clara and the Nutcracker. It was her mother's favourite, too, Amelie told me, before she went backstage.

Gayatri squeezed my hand; my eyes glistened. I'd asked her who Rajni was, and she'd told me she was Amelie's mother. It all fitted – the warning from Madeleine, Rahul's mention of responsibility. He was Amelie's guardian because of his friendship with Rajni. Amelie's mother was not dead, as I'd assumed, but alive and living in France.

After the show, we went back to the house for late dinner, and the phone rang as we were clearing up in the kitchen. Amelie rushed to pick it up. She spoke animatedly to Rahul, explaining the applause and how people had stood up. Then she turned to hand the phone to me, saying that I would be better able to explain her performance.

I took the phone off her, chest aching. Would he talk to me like nothing had happened? Would he go back to the aloofness he'd adopted before?

Instead, I heard him release a low breath and then he hung up. The intermittent tone stabbed sharply at my already fragile heart. Hot stinging tears rolled down my face and I ran into the bathroom.

He couldn't speak with me. We'd ruined everything, and we'd have no more professional or civil conversation. The atmosphere would be tense when he was home in Richmond. I would have to let go, let go of my relationship with Amelie.

I won't stop you from seeing Amelie or Ma. I can see how much they mean to you.

But his behaviour would stop me if he avoided me like this.

I held my arms around myself for comfort. The tears wouldn't stop. I'd thought I was beyond the excruciating pain, the hurt of loving a man who would never love me the same.

When I came out of the bathroom, Gayatri was in the lounge. She picked up the teapot and filled my cup with chai.

"Amelie went to her room, you can go see her before you leave."

I couldn't stop my hands from shaking as I held the teacup.

"What happened between you two?"

I continued to stare at the tea in my cup. Gayatri's kind eyes fixed on my face. I knew I wouldn't be able to keep my hurt from showing.

"Nothing, we had a bit of an argument. And I've been sick."

Frowning, she told me off for coming out and not resting. "There's more, do you want to tell me?"

I let the tears flood out again and told her that I was going to Preston to tell my aunt and uncle that I couldn't marry Niraj. I explained how I would be living a lie if I continued seeing him. I left out the part that I'd been stupid enough to think that Rahul and I had a future together.

⸫TWENTY NINE⸪

RAHUL STOOD at the entrance to the sitting room. Mini had answered the insistent door chimes minutes earlier. My stomach lurched through my windpipe and nearly choked me. *What is he doing in Preston? Why is he at my childhood home?*

Why did he look so traumatised and unkempt, his pristine clothes crumpled, his eyes sad and surrounded by dark circles, a five o'clock shadow on his chin, the glistening hair with greying sideburns dishevelled? I knew Gayatri and Amelie were safe, I'd spoken to them last night to confirm that what I was about to do was right. At least right for me and right for Niraj.

When I'd met with Niraj the week Rahul had left me, he'd been cautious, his usually chatty demeanour subdued. But when I had told him how I felt about Rahul, he had smiled and told me he'd known there was someone else and had wondered why I'd agreed to meet with him. Niraj was a perceptive and kind man. In the time I'd spent with him, I knew I'd found a loyal friend. Someone who would support me. So, when I decided to tell my family we wouldn't be getting married, he insisted on coming up to Preston with me.

"No ifs, no buts," he'd said, when I protested. We'd come on the early train, Niraj, Mini and I. Dennis was already up for the weekend and Niraj and I had gathered in the living room to uncouple. To tell my aunt and uncle that we would no longer be seeing each other.

The atmosphere was tense. I'd told my family of the decision I'd made about my future, how I'd fallen in love with someone else. That if I married, I would only ever marry for love. Chanda Mami hadn't said a word, but her eyes had blazed with anger.

Then Rahul had showed up, without warning.

"Good afternoon." Rahul shook Kalpesh Mama's hand, then shook hands with Dennis and Niraj in the sitting room.

Chanda Mami fisted her hands and stared daggers in my direction.

"Can I speak with you in private, Hema?" he said.

"No, I don't think so," Mami reprimanded. "Have you no shame? You seduced a young girl. Someone who worked for you. You filled her head with luv shuv."

I startled. How had Chanda Mami guessed it was Rahul that I'd fallen in love with? Mini was the only one who knew. Except I'd told Niraj and he must have told Dennis

I threw a questioning stare at Dennis, who avoided meeting my eyes.

Chanda Mami whirled on me. "And shame on you, besharam, for coming here and telling us that the boy we have found for you is not acceptable. That you are in love with someone else. This boy—" she pointed, "—this boy has agreed to accept you with your disfigurement."

Niraj winced. Mini's jaw tightened. Dennis straightened, and Kalpesh Mama stepped closer to the pair.

Rahul's fist clenched as he towered over my aunt. "How dare you? How can you say that of Hema? She is beautiful. Her scars are full of beauty."

Mini smirked at me.

Chanda Mami held his gaze. "How old are you, Rahul?"

"Thirty-eight." He frowned.

"Why are you behaving like a child? You are old enough to understand that Niraj is right for Hema. He is—" She pursed her lips. She'd been about to say he was disabled, too, that he also had a handicap. *Poor Hema and poor Niraj with his discreet hearing aids. Who will marry Niraj if Hema won't accept him?*

"What do you know about Rahul, Hema?" Chandi Mami asked.

I jittered with shock as she glared contemptuously at him. My mami had taken a dislike to Rahul since we'd met at the restaurant, and she had made it a point to mention that I should not see the Raichuras again.

"Why aren't you married?" she demanded.

Everyone averted their gaze and stared intently at the carpet. She stood up abruptly, her dark eyes sharp, and asked about his time in France, his many trips abroad, his inability to find a wife, his relationship with a child who was not related to him.

The words were like tiny pebbles aimed at his soul. "Do you have a secret woman, Rahul? Is she housed somewhere away from prying eyes? The mother of your child? The child you say isn't yours?"

His eyes glazed with pain.

"Chanda!" Kalpesh Mama pulled her towards the kitchen. "Be quiet. Rahul, you and Hema can talk in my office."

"Well, haven't you wondered, Kalpesh, why he brought the child to live with him? What dirty past does he have?" she added as they walked into the kitchen.

I asked Rahul to follow me, but instead of leading him to the office, I stepped out into the back garden and walked to the end. I needed some fresh air to stop my lungs from bursting. I needed to understand why he had come to northern England.

"What did she mean by luv shuv? Why are you here?" he said.

I stared at the pale-yellow roses cascading down the arbour. Their scent mingled with the heady mix of his aftershave: cedarwood, juniper and mint. The skin stretched on the back of my neck. *Why is he in Preston? He had taken a post in Paris to be with Rajni.*

His body turned towards me. I closed my eyes.

"Open your eyes. Hema, look at me, please tell me."

I looked. Instead of the clouded cold eyes, I found a soulful gaze. "I came to tell my family the truth."

"Truth? Why isn't Niraj's family here?" He grabbed my fist and loosened it, lacing his fingers in mine. My hands warmed to his touch. "Aren't you announcing your engagement today?"

My head rocked from side to side in denial.

He raked through his hair and stared at me. "But Ma said—" His lips fluttered, and a grin grew on his face. He guided me to sit under the arbour.

My legs were glad of the relief. He informed me that being away from me had been the worst days of his life. He explained how he found the earliest flight out of Paris. He spoke of the anxiety-filled journey into Birmingham and the drive up the motorway at breakneck speed to stop the announcement. To declare his love.

I rested my head on his shoulder as he spoke, my chest filling with a tingling sensation. I stored the moment in the box of memories that held my time with him.

We sat under the rose-infused arbour as his body relaxed and his heart quieted beneath my ear.

"Your mami doesn't like me," he said as he lifted my chin.

I informed him my mami hadn't liked Niraj, either, but had been grateful to him for accepting me and my disfigurement.

He put his finger to my lips. "Don't say that. You are beautiful, and your scarred body is who you are. Never repeat those words. Will you marry me, Hema?"

He fell to his knees, clasping my hand. I wanted to say yes, but my mami's words resounded in my ears. *The mother of your child. The child you say isn't yours.*

"Get up, I want the truth. Whose child is Amelie? Is she yours?"

His shoulders fell forward. He pulled himself to sit next to me and recounted his time in Paris in the heady nineties.

"I told you that Rajni and I worked together. We worked in two different divisions, but our paths crossed frequently. Rajni was the belle of Marseille; her charisma and natural charm seduced all who came into her sphere. It was my fault she became sick. We had finished working on an enormous deal, long hours, no sleep. Everyone did drugs then. I dabbled, but not as regularly as some of my colleagues. Rajni took it to the next level. She needed drugs to stay awake and drugs to help her sleep. I couldn't get what she wanted from my usual supplier, so I found someone else. We got a bad batch; it tripped us over the edge. Ma and Mukesh Uncle came to visit me in the hospital. I recovered quickly, but Rajni stayed in the hospital for weeks. Ma stayed by her bedside. I… she was my girlfriend."

I had always known that she was more than a friend, but the word 'girlfriend' pierced my soul. *He cared about her, and he still loves her.*

He wouldn't ever love me the way he loved her. He'd rushed back to help her, even when he'd known she would hurt him. That type of love only came once. *He can't love me the same way.*

"If Rajni is Amelie's mother, is Amelie?" I asked, my head hanging, my heart thrashing in my chest. Rahul was harbouring a secret. Something about his need to protect Amelie felt odd. The words *my Amelie* drifted into my mind. She must be his child.

"Yes, but I swear I didn't know she was pregnant. When Rajni became seriously ill, she thought everyone was out to harm her. She was always quick to temper, but it got worse. I couldn't stay with her; she hated me; she wanted to hurt me. That's how I got the wounds. Ma was terrified that one day she'd find me dead. I asked for a transfer to London."

He moves away. I understood why he had gone off to New York and Paris. It was his coping mechanism. If I said yes, would he run away if things got tough?

"Ma doesn't like it when I disappear to Paris, but I'm Rajni's only next-of-kin. She has no one, Hema. Madeleine helps as often as she can, but she has ailing parents. I've made Rajni the way she is. It is all my fault." He held his head in his hands. "You won't want to marry me now, you'll hate me. Hate me for deserting her."

The thrashing in my chest stopped. I wanted to be with him more than anyone in the world, even if he had responsibilities for Rajni and Amelie. I loved Amelie like my own child. How could I hate the woman who was her mother, and how could I hate Rahul? He hadn't abandoned her. He hadn't left her to cope on her own.

I took his hands. "I don't hate you."

His eyes softened and his lips lifted.

"Rajni loves Ma. When Amelie was three, she wrote to Ma and told her she had a grandchild. Ma helped Rajni to join a programme, found Céleste as Amelie's full-time caregiver, and things got better. I pay for everything, and I want you to know that. Rajni's money has gone. She's slipped back into the illness; the episodes have become more frequent. She has moments of lucidity when she charms and convinces people to let her out. That's how she came to Aix." He paused and stared into the garden.

I remembered the wound and my heart fidgeted with fright. "Does she hurt Amelie?" I couldn't bear the thought of the little girl in pain.

"No, no, my dil, she only hates me. She thinks I'm a monster, the monster who brought on her illness. The monster who's taken away her freedom." He pulled me to his side. "My name is not on her birth certificate, but Amelie is my child. Rajni won't let us tell her. I can't wait, wait for Rajni to tell Amelie the truth of her birth. Your mami is right; I have a secret life. Do you still love me and want to be with me, after knowing of Rajni and Amelie?"

He wiped at his face, his eyes haunted from the memories of his past life, his hands shielding his pain. I pulled them away and kissed them.

His eyebrows scrunched. "I've done it again. I don't have a ring." He let go of my grip and walked to the border and plucked out a piece of couch grass and twisted and turned it.

He knelt at my feet. "Hemanshi Pattni, will you be my wife?" His lips curled and the grin stretched to his eyes.

His smile turned my knees to mush and made my belly flip and flop. My skin tingled as goosebumps raised like a Mexican wave all over my body. I had dreamt of this day so many times. The world where Rahul, Amelie and I were a family. I hadn't counted on Rajni being part of it, but I knew that I would not deprive Amelie of a relationship with her mother.

"Yes, yes. But promise you won't go strange on me again."

He lifted me. "You have all my secrets, my dil."

We kissed, hidden from prying eyes, although I was sure Chanda Mami was on the stool, spying on us from the kitchen window.

THIRTY

MAMI'S SHORT, STOUT frame turned as we stepped back into the house. Her eyes narrowed as she saw our entwined hands, and she hurriedly followed us to the living room.

My mama asked me to join him in the office. Rahul let go of my hand reluctantly and walked cautiously to the vacated armchair. I slipped the makeshift ring off my finger and inserted it in the back pocket of my jeans as I climbed up the stairs behind my uncle.

My heart thudded against my ribs; my uncle's expression was stern, his usually upturned lips forming a straight line.

"Sit." He pointed to the chair opposite his dark wooden desk.

My throat felt like sandpaper as I tried to swallow. The ticking grandfather clock grew louder. For the first time in my life, I was frightened of my lovely, gentle uncle. He unlocked a drawer and pulled out a large red folder and laid it in front of him, his fingers laced together, his hands resting on top.

He slumped. "I was waiting for your twenty-fifth birthday to show you this. But Rahul turning up today has made it important that you learn about this." He tapped the folder with his index finger. "This… is your investment portfolio. When your family passed away, I had to take charge of all your assets."

He pushed the folder towards me. I opened it. On the first page was an account summary. I had to read the figures twice. My breath caught and my chest tightened. The sound of the clock faded.

There I was scrimping and saving for my travels, cautious with my money, and I had this amount the whole time? I glanced up, my hand over my mouth. Kind eyes glistened back at me.

"It's a substantial amount. There's enough interest there to buy a decent property in London, and, if you carry on with the investment, a nice little income to add to your travel fund. Or you could give up working in a job that doesn't make you happy, and do what you're good at, teaching. I set up the trust to grow your parent's portfolio. Kartik was a shrewd investor. He taught me all I know about the stock market. Did I tell you that before?"

I shook my head and he paused. His eyes glazed as they drifted to a spot on the wall behind me. His face softened as he relived a memory of my parents.

I had seen him do this so many times. The softness would disappear soon, and a pain would wash over him.

He held his palm to his chest. "You can't have access to it until your twenty-fifth birthday." His voice choked.

I picked up a buff folder with an Indian stamp and flicked through to allow him time to compose himself. An ache grew in my chest. "What's this?"

"That's your grandparent's property. I have had to get someone to look after it. He's a good man; he's kept it in excellent condition. All the expenses are in there. When you're ready to see it or if you want to sell it, I can put you in touch with a lawyer. I couldn't liquidate your assets in India. Thank God your parents were astute and had a will. It made—" His voice wavered, and he stopped and stared at me as tears filled his eyes and he fumbled in his pocket for a handkerchief.

I couldn't bear to see my uncle cry. He rarely did it in front of me, but in that moment, he finally allowed me to see his suffering. A heaviness filled my heart. He had lost his only sibling, my mother, and his nephews and best friend.

He saw that the news had overwhelmed me as I took halting breaths. He lifted me from my chair and held me.

"Too many truths in one day." He stroked my head. "Take a deep breath, dikri." He grabbed a tissue and gave it to me. "I'll leave you for a bit."

"Don't… go." I stammered.

Kalpesh Mama sat on the chair and tugged me to his lap. "I'm sorry, I have been a useless parent to you. I let my wife mistreat you. You do know I love you."

I nodded. I loved my mama. I loved that he sat me on his lap and stroked my head to comfort me, as he had always done. I was the only one he had ever done that to. It had made me feel special when I was growing up, knowing that unique experience was mine and mine alone.

All this time, he had been quietly building my fortune, planning a comfortable life. I cried into his shoulder until the moisture drained out of my eyes. I thanked him, and he shook his head, tears rolling down his cheek. I kissed him where the wet tracks ran. I pulled out the makeshift ring.

His eyes narrowed, then an enormous smile filled his face. "So, he's finally asked?"

I frowned at him.

"I could see that he loved you when we met him at Veeraswamy. It just took Rahul a little longer to accept."

***

AS WE APPROACHED the staircase, Rahul was pacing at the bottom, the same way he had when he'd waited for me in Aix. His head lifted to us and lines appeared on his forehead.

I smiled. His lips twitched, and the twitch grew into a broad, radiant smile. I held Kalpesh Mama's arm tighter for support.

In the sitting room, the others sat in pairs, mother and son on the small sofa, Niraj and Mini on the larger one. No one was talking.

Kalpesh Mama walked in and announced that I was a very wealthy young woman and if I chose not to marry Niraj, he would support me.

I looked across to Niraj. He smirked and turned his head to Mini, who beamed back. Something was going on between the two that tugged at my consciousness. Then I remembered the conversation the night Dennis had introduced us and how Mini had gushed about him.

"How stupid of me," I told myself under my breath.

"Did you say something, my dil?" Rahul whispered.

"Nothing," I said, grinning.

"What took you so long, Kalpesh? This... this man wants to ask us something." Chanda Mami stood up and pointed at Rahul. "And Niraj, Meena and he have been huddled in gup shup. I don't know what's going on, come sit down." She pulled at him, then pointed me towards the space next to Dennis.

My mama pulled me to his side and looked scornfully at his wife. "I've told Hema she is a wealthy woman, Chanda, and that she need not work for a living."

I watched my aunt's mouth open and close as the news of my inheritance dawned on her.

Dennis pulled me away from his father and embraced me. "You really are like Harry Potter, H.P. How much gold do you have stored in Gringotts?"

I laughed.

Chanda Mami gave me a seething look. "You can joke as much as you like, but I want to know what this man wants."

Rahul cleared his throat, and Kalpesh Mama took my hand and put it in Rahul's.

His wife shrieked. "Kalpesh, what have you done?

THIRTY ONE

We were sitting in the garden, drinking tea, the scent of lavender making me reminisce of our time in the South of France.

"Are you nervous?" I asked.

My family were coming to meet with the Raichuras to announce our betrothal, a simple ceremony of our intent to marry involving a glass of sweetened milk and an exchange of clothes and rings.

"I want your mami to like my family. I'm not sure how she will react to the announcements tonight."

"Don't be, she's changed. She was nice to me at Mini's birthday meal."

Rahul took a sip from his cup. A twitch lifted the corner of his mouth. "Did Niraj come?"

I told him of the lack of reaction from my aunt at Niraj being there, too, but I had an uneasiness in my stomach, my words of reassurance a false hope. Earlier in the morning, I'd seen Céleste talking to a small woman in a hooded top in the garden, but she had sneered when I mentioned it and told me I was mistaken. My mistrust of Céleste grew the more time I spent with her. But how could I deny Amelie her main caregiver? The woman who had helped her mother when she needed it the most?

Gayatri and Mukesh were announcing the Jaimala ceremony at the Sanatan Dharma Mandir in Cardiff in the evening. The Raichuras were an extremely tolerant bunch, and I understood Rahul's nerves. My family were conventional, although so much had changed since that day in Preston, I was genuinely unsure of Chanda Mami's reaction.

He pulled at my free hand. "Are you nervous, my dil?"

We were going to explain what the ceremony meant to Amelie so she understood who I would become before the ritual tonight. I took a deep breath. "Yes, I love Amelie, but I don't want her to choose. I'm more than happy to be called Hema. I know I'll be a good mother to her, no matter what she calls me."

"You, my dil, have been more than that. You are a friend, a confidant and a mother. My daughter is lucky to have you in her life." He lifted my hand to his lips.

"*Tonton*, Ema, look at my hair." Amelie ran up to us and lifted herself onto my lap.

"Goodness, *ma pitchounette*, you are like a pari." Rahul nibbled on her knuckles, making her squeal.

"I have curls just like yours, Ema." Amelie patted her head, a gesture she had picked up from her grandmother. She talked about the little hat with the hose she had to wear. "We had to wait for so long. Did you know *Mémé* has tea and biscuits at the salon? I had juice and biscuits. You should have come, Ema."

Rahul cleared his throat. He'd gone back to Paris after the surprise visit to Preston and spoken to Rajni, who'd agreed to an official adoption. To give Amelie the recognition as Rahul's child.

She stopped, and her head darted from me to him and back again. I gave her a nod. As he explained that he was her father, her mouth fell open and her shiny eyes sought mine for confirmation.

"Does that mean you are my *papa?*" She frowned, tapping her finger on her lip. "You do know *papa* have to buy their children everything?"

He chuckled. "Yes, I do."

She clapped. "Can I have a scooter? I've always wanted one, please, please." She held her palms together and fluttered her eyelashes.

Rahul lifted her onto his lap. "You can have anything you want as long as you call me *Papa.*"

"Okay, *Papa*, I'll make a list."

He kissed her on her forehead.

"Today's the best day ever. Mukesh *Oncle* will be my new *papi,* and you are my *papa.*"

"One more thing, jinki dikri."

My uneasiness grew. The hairs on the back of my neck rose. I turned around to see if anyone was watching. Rahul squeezed my hand.

"Your *papa* and I are getting married," I said. "So if you want to… you can call me *Maman.*"

She frowned and considered the news.

"I love you, Amelie. If you don't want to, it doesn't matter." My heart ached at her anxiety. If I had been asked to make a choice when I was younger, I would not have wanted to call my mami Mummy.

"But I love *Maman,*" she said.

"Your *maman* will always be your *maman, ma pitchounette.* This ceremony we are having today is to announce that Hema will be my wife, we will be a proper family. You could call her *maman* too."

She grinned and squealed again, clapping. "I'm happy, very happy. I have a *Grand-père,* and two *Maman,* one in France and one here in England." She jumped off Rahul's lap and ran into the living room, shouting. "I have to tell *Mémé, Tata* and Maya."

I felt a chill on the back of my neck again and turned to the end of the garden. Rahul drew me up into his arms. "It wasn't that bad, my dil. She loves you."

So why was there a feeling of queasiness in my stomach? *Why does every cell in my body fill with foreboding?* My family's reaction to Rahul's official adoption of Amelie and Gayatri's wedding couldn't be creating the dread that rooted my feet.

"Will you tell Rajni about us?"

"Of course. When I see her again, I'll tell her about our marriage and that Ma and Mukesh Uncle are getting married. She has a right to know."

He lifted my face. Our mouths met, and his soft lips filled me with so much love that my heart quieted. The uneasiness seeped away and I savoured his kisses, his luscious lips on mine, the rise and fall of pleasure in my stomach. I inhaled; the odour of him and the perfume of lavender calmed me down. A little.

THIRTY TWO

A NOISE FROM Amelie's room woke me. The excitement of the evening and the lack of any drama after the two announcements about Gayatri's wedding and Rahul's adoption had resulted in a pleasurable evening. The Jogia and Raichura family had found common ground regarding the people they knew from their life in East Africa.

Most surprising of all had been my aunt's behaviour. She no longer sneered at any compliments delivered to me. Even when Mini and Niraj had left together, my aunt had not reacted, neither had she reacted to me staying for the weekend. *If only Kalpesh Mama had put his foot down sooner, perhaps Mini and I would have had a better time growing up.*

Dim flickering lights danced on the carpet in the hallway. My stomach quivered with fear, a terror that had taken hold in my sleep.

"You think you can take my baby away from me," came a voice from Amelie's bedroom. The woman spoke in French, her unfamiliar voice hushed.

I hesitated outside the bedroom door.

"No, no. I don't." There was a nervous edge to Rahul's voice. "I'm taking care of Amelie until you get better. Do you remember, Rajni? You called Ma to help you."

"No, keep away, keep away. *Bébé*, wake up, wake up, *Maman* is here."

I stepped into Amelie's room. The stranger's head turned towards me. There was something familiar about her, her stature, the way she held her chin out. Her long black dress, the way her straight hair hung down her back. She barely reached Rahul's chest and yet she oozed menace.

That's when I saw the kitchen knife. The flickering lights of the candles shimmered on the sharp blade.

Suddenly, memories of her appeared like an apparitions. She was the woman who'd loitered around the house in Aix. She was Rajni Amin, Amelie's mother.

My lungs ached for breath and my eyes searched for any sign of harm in the two people who meant everything to me.

Rahul said, "Go back to your room, Hema." His eyes were full of fear, the sound of his voice hollow.

Amelie sat up in bed and hugged her mother. The flickering lights of the candelabra danced in her sleepy eyes. "*Maman*, you came. Céleste said you would." She sought Rahul and me. "Look, *Tonton*, Ema, look. *Maman's* come to fetch me." She covered her mouth, her hand shaking. "Sorry, you're my *papa* and *maman* too." She peered warily at her mother.

Rajni's expression remained the same, but her knuckles whitened on the handle of the kitchen knife.

Amelie's bottom lip quivered as she saw the knife. Her chin wobbled, and my heart broke. I had the urge to comfort her. But I sensed that if I rushed forward, Rajni could hurt her. I stepped into the room slowly, my instinct to protect Amelie overwhelming, my eardrums bursting with the irregular thud of my heartbeat.

Rajni thrusted the blade at me. "Keep away."

I raised my hands up to show my harmlessness and swallowed several times to push down the taste of fear. "Amelie, let's get your bags ready, your *maman* has come to fetch you."

Rahul stepped a little closer to Rajni, a sheen of sweat on his forehead.

"Stay where you are, Rahul. Let your fiancée— she is your fiancée—do her job." Rajni stood up. "Stop crying, *Bébé*. We are going home."

Tears streamed down Amelie's face and she whimpered like a frightened animal.

"Mind what you're doing."

Rajni's eyes narrowed and she moved closer to Rahul. "I'm not afraid to use this. You're pathetic, Rahul. How old is this girl? Twenty? Couldn't you find a woman?" She sneered.

A trickle of sweat ran down the side of his face as his eyes pleaded for me to leave.

I couldn't. I wouldn't leave the two people who meant the world to me. *Think, Hema. How can you calm her down enough to release the knife?* My group therapy sessions with people who'd suffered a trauma flashed before me. I just needed to stay calm and do as Rajni bade. I hoped Rahul would understand my intentions.

I walked cautiously to the wardrobe and reached for the little pink suitcase on top. "Amelie, come and choose what you want to take with you." My heart thumped uncontrollably, but I tried to keep my voice light and cheery.

Amelie's eyes pleaded with her mother for permission to get out of bed.

"Go, *Bébé*, find some nice clothes. We are staying with *Tata* in Marseille."

I froze on the spot. Madeleine was helping Rajni? How could she? She was Rahul's friend as much as Rajni's. What had made her support a woman who clearly needed help?

"Stay still, Rahul." Rajni pressed the tip of the knife to his waist; a small red stain appeared on his T-shirt. "No tricks, Hema. If you do anything, I'll stick this in him. I've done it before, and I'll do it again."

All I wanted to do was pounce on the woman, grab the knife out of her hand to protect my love, but Rahul shook his head a fraction.

"I... I'm... I promise, I'm only helping Amelie."

Rahul's eyes clouded. His cheeks greyed and his hands hung by his sides as he held Rajni's gaze.

Amelie tugged at my pyjama top; I tried to reassure her with my eyes, hoping she could see the calmness I needed to display.

Once I'd filled the bag, I asked if I could go with Amelie to the dresser. As I turned to walk towards the cupboard, Amelie tripped. Rajni's hand lowered, her forehead furrowed.

"*Bébé*, are you hurt?"

Rahul took advantage of Rajni's distraction to prise the blade out of her grasp, the handle in his palm. But she was stronger than her petite build suggested and she pushed at him, turning the knife. The blade lodged in his stomach.

Rajni lurched backward and toppled the candelabra on the desk behind her. The flimsy curtains flamed. Rahul slumped onto his knees and shouted through gritted teeth as Rajni towered over him.

"Run!" he roared. "Save Amelie."

I pulled Amelie onto my hip and ran out of the room as the hammock of soft toys above the desk ignited into a wall of flames.

The fire alarm sounded as I clamoured downstairs. Gayatri and Mukesh came out of their rooms. I yelled that the house was on fire and told everyone to get out. I pushed Amelie into her grandmother's chest, prying her arms away from my neck. "You're safe, go with *Mémé*."

"Hema, Hema, come back," Gayatri yelled as I ran back up to the bedroom.

The acrid stink of burnt plastic filled my throat, and I stretched my pyjama top to cover my mouth. Furious flames reached the ceiling.

Rajni's clothes were aflame. Her guttural shrieks echoed through my body. Rahul was swaying on his feet; Rajni had pushed him against the burning wall, her arms clamped around him.

Instinct took over. Adrenaline surged through my veins. The flames grew hotter as I searched frantically for something to hurt Rajni with, for a way to protect Rahul.

"She's mine! SHE'S MINE!" she screamed at him, her long hair melted into a black helmet.

I grabbed the small dressing table chair and hit her on the head. She fell into a crumbled heap at Rahul's feet. His T-shirt had gone, revealing black and red blisters on his chest. The knife was still lodged in his stomach. My nostrils burnt from the choking smoke and cooked flesh.

I pulled him out, slamming the bedroom door shut. I grabbed the flower vase on the landing table and wet his torso. It did nothing to the flames. My hands pulled at what remained of his clothes, patting out the fire.

He stared at me, emotionless, and collapsed.

"Think, Hema think! What should you do?"

Suddenly, the rules I'd seen in the fire safety films flashed in front of my eyes. I had to cool him down—the first rule of burn treatment. Douse the burn by drenching it in cold water.

I ran to the bathroom, emptied the bucket that held Amelie's toys, and soaked him with water, one bucket after another. It was a futile gesture; I could see the blisters grow in front of my eyes and knew it wasn't enough.

"Please, please, Rahul, please stay with me." Tears blurred my vision. Someone shouted.

"It's okay. We're here, love." They pulled the bucket out of my hand.

The adrenaline depleted and my body become boneless. I sat on the wet, carpeted floor, unable to do or say anything.

The sense of dread I had been holding all day was leading to this moment. Rahul's burns were serious; his upper body had the largest exposed area of skin, and his chest was blistering red and black. The handle of a knife protruded from his stomach.

I knew that the dread had been a warning. A warning that I would lose the man I loved.

The hallway began to spin. The shouting abated, and darkness came.

'THIRTY THREE'

"HE'S A FIGHTER, he won't leave us," Gayatri said, reaching for me. Her shoulders slumped as she saw my hands. "When will they take the bandages off?"

"Tomorrow, they are almost healed." I was in turmoil. My burns were nothing compared to Rahul's.

The man I was in love with, the man who I was going to marry, was hooked up to tubes and machines, his burns so acute the doctors had put him into an induced coma. My nightmares had returned, but instead of children kicking and screaming at me, I saw Rajni clinging to both Rahul and Amelie as flames rose and engulfed them.

Gayatri had come every day to Chelsea and Westminster Hospital. She arrived at nine and stayed until the end of the school day, encouraging me to eat and drink, helping with my hand exercises. Rahul and I were both in the same unit. My bed was in the main ward and Rahul's in the intensive care room on the other side of the glass partition, I stared through every minute of my waking day.

I had no recollection of what had happened after the fire brigade had come that night. When I'd woken up, my family were waiting for me – the way they had done so many times in my childhood. Kalpesh Mama had filled me in on Rahul's condition. The doctors had put him into a drug-induced coma so they could scrape and remove all the dead and burnt skin. He had sustained burns to his chest, back and arms, forty percent of his skin's surface.

Forty percent wasn't as bad as some of the children I had helped in my support group. My first set of burns had only been eighteen percent, but a lot had changed in burn treatment since my childhood injury. Artificial skin grafts sped up recovery; tight clothing helped blood flow. But the most dangerous aspects of Rahul's recovery were the germs, the micro bacteria, the E. coli and the streptococcus. The highest risk was sepsis. If that happened, blood pressure dropped. Body temperature rose and organs failed as the body succumbed to septic shock.

Risk of infection kept us outside the room. I wanted to hold his hands, to show him I was there. His hands, his beautiful long fingers, were clenched and bound into white stumps. I longed to have them trace the scars on my body again.

***

MY DISCHARGE CAME a week later. I left armed with detailed instructions on how to apply the antibiotic creams and cleanse, protect and elevate my burnt hands. Not that I needed them. I knew the routine.

But I didn't leave. I insisted on being with Rahul at the hospital. I only left to sleep and freshen up for a few hours, then spent all my time waiting at his bedside.

Machines and tubes assisted his survival, his breathing aided by a device, his body temperature controlled by a heated mattress, various cannulas added for the intravenous drips. I became used to the sounds, the hisses, the bleeps and squeaky wheels on trolleys. The cacophony of noise brought back memories of my frequent stays in hospitals.

At least here no one saw me as a freak, someone who needed to be pitied. At least in the burns unit, there were people like me, my group, my people. The nurses and doctors became used to me, knowing that I was a survivor of a similar injury, knowing that they had to be honest with me. He needed to have several skin grafts, long operations that filled me with dread; each one came with the risk that he would die. Some skin grafts took, others didn't, and we waited, and I waited, waited for my love to show signs of coming back to me.

Every time I left, my chest constricted and the thought of losing him overwhelmed me. *What if he leaves me, who will love me like that again? How will I live without him?*

Amelie, our sweet little girl, sent drawings of her day for her *papa*, and I would describe them to him, explaining the scenes, hoping he could hear me.

When I first came home, I checked on her to make sure she had coped with the trauma of that night. Her nightmares were worse, and she clung to me, unable to let me out of her sight.

I spoke with my support group and found help. We found someone to help her, and she began to draw pictures of how she felt; at first, they were full of dark clouds and monsters that entered her room while she slept. Slowly, she sketched everyday scenes. Ma – that was what I called Gayatri now – told me of the night terrors, Amelie's reluctance to sleep alone. My poor Amelie's sleep was full of the two people she had lost: Céleste and her mother.

Céleste had been told to pack her bags and leave. Mukesh and Ma felt betrayed by her duplicitous dealing with them. She had encouraged Rajni, aided her in her plan to take Amelie away.

No one ventured to the upper floors; my room was smoke-damaged, Amelie's bedroom destroyed along with the dolls, the clothes, the little tutus and the dressing-up boxes. A tarpaulin covered the stairs and barred our access. I slept in my lover's room, filling myself with his scent, with the aftershave that lingered on his clothes. My sleep came with the aid of drugs, utterly devoid of dreams, a temporary respite from my day. But my days were filled with nightmares, every waking hour replete with dread and despair.

***

THE DAY FOR MA'S planned wedding came and passed. The long, hot month of July passed, and Rahul's eyebrows grew back. The face of the man I loved came back. But he lay like a corpse, his eyes closed.

We played his favourite music. I grew to love his favourite Hindi songs as much as he did. I listened to Robert Palmer for the first time in my life. I discovered that the lead singer of The Communards was a man. *Who'd have thought after listening to their songs?*

Debjani came to visit and teased him about the time he had followed her like a lost puppy. Of the constant quotes from "Kabhi Kabhie" that he'd left for her. I memorised the lyrics and songs, too, and sang them to him when everyone had gone home, hoping my voice would bring him back to me.

I learnt of the antics of his childhood in Kampala, of his years at school and university. His partners came and spoke of their first big deal and updates on their work. The art dealer wrote to tell me about his first art purchases. We received so much mail I was inundated with writing thank-you notes.

Rahul Raichura had helped so many people. I was proud to have found him, to have found someone who had comforted so many. I understood the reason he had helped Rajni; it was not guilt. I learnt that what had started as guilt had turned into a need to give back for his good fortune. I began to pray every day, light a divo to appeal to Krishna to save my love.

* * *

ONE MONTH LATER, the plastic surgeons reduced the drugs, and I made plans to stay with Rahul in his room until he woke up. As the hospital quieted, desperation pained my heart. What if he never woke up, never came back to me?

I began to talk as if my life depended on him hearing my words, words to stop him from slipping away from me. I told him how much I loved him, of when I fell in love with him. I recalled the day I'd realized that he was the person I had been searching for all my life.

I told him of my regret at my response to our first kiss. The night he told me I was made for him, the lyrics from his favourite song, "Ke... tujko banaya gaya."

·THIRTY FOUR

"DO YOU REMEMBER when you waited for me that morning at Aix, the day we drove to the reservoir? I was dreading it. I haven't told you this before. I've been trying to make sense of it. I dreamt of meeting you. I saw your face before I met you. Isn't that strange? The dreams started while I was living in Paris. Were you there, Rahul? Is that why I dreamt of you? I'm not a romantic. How could I be? All my life people have treated me as a freak. Someone who needed pity. A person who would be lucky to find love. All my boyfriends have known of my disfigurement; I know you don't like me to use that word, but I will continue using it until you tell me not to. Is it making you angry, Rahul? I'm disfigured. You've seen my body; it's not perfect." A sob caught in my throat at the thought of the protective clothes that covered his body. At the body that would be scarred like mine. I wanted to lie with him and hold him in the metal bed, but I sat on a hard plastic chair, unable to hold his scarred hand. Afraid I would hurt him.

"When I saw the advert in 'The Lady', you invaded my dreams again, and I knew I was meant for the job. I was so cross when I left the house that day.

Cross because your voice had pierced me, cross I would not meet with you face-to-face. After the interview, I sulked all the way to Mini's, unable to understand why I was devastated at not getting an au pair job. It had happened to me before. But when I met Ma, I had found a home. I told myself I was stupid; I had only known your mother for few hours. When you called me, my heart pounded, and your voice filled me up. Can that happen? Can a voice vibrate through every cell in your body and expand? When Mini and I came to drop off the contract, I was afraid. I dared not examine the photos, you know, the ones on display in the sitting room. When I think of that day, I knew, I knew you were the man of my dreams."

I gasped for air as I thought of the missed opportunity. I should have examined the photographs and told Mini. She would have told me off when I'd asked Rahul to keep his distance, told me that he was my destiny. She believed in a greater power sending a sign.

"That night, when you almost ran me over, I was shocked, shocked to see you outside my dreams, shocked that we were in Aix together. I spent the rest of that evening wondering how I could find you. Imagine my surprise when you revealed your face. My heart pounded so much that morning. I felt I would die from a heart attack. It took all my strength to stay upright, to go to my room. Do you think like that too? Can anyone feel like that? Then your lips curled up, and I saw your radiant smile, Rahul, and it hollowed me out, drained me of all my energy. I felt light-headed. Am I addicted to you? Am I addicted to your dazzling smile? Please, wake up and show me your smile again. I bask in the glory of your grin. I feel whole. I feel beautiful. Stay with me, please stay."

The thought of losing him overwhelmed me. Tears burnt tracks on my cheeks and I stood up to brush his soft new hair away from his forehead. To touch him, to let him feel my touch.

"That was the first day I knew I was in love with you, Rahul, the day we left to view Mont Victoire. But I had doubts, too. Can anybody fall in love with a dream? I doubted my dream. I told myself that you weren't that man, that I'd made you that man. I had to ignore my feelings. It was not professional of me to make you my lover. So I kept my distance, I stayed away, although I wanted to linger in your presence, to listen to your voice as it settled in my stomach. I watched you with Amelie, how you comforted her when she was sad, how you told her funny stories that made her laugh. She loves you, she misses you, please wake up for her sake."

I had to stop. My throat choked. I loved Amelie; she had lost her mother, the mother who had now become a monster of her dreams. *What if she loses her father too? What if he never wakes up?*

I would lose her too, then. I had no legal claim on her. My name was not on the adoption papers.

I slumped on the chair, unable to speak, the space in my chest sore. I fell silent for a while.

"My distancing made my dreams worse. You came to me every night, your lips kissing mine, your body pinning mine. I dreamt of how you laughed at me when you saw me playing and joking with Amelie. My subconscious created a life with you, with Amelie, with Ma. I became part of your life. That's why I agreed to be your tennis partner. I wanted to add memories to the fantasy world I lived in my sleep. I wish I had told you how I felt.

"Do you remember the night we celebrated our win? The night you told me you loved me? That night is etched in my brain. I can tell you every moment. I can describe what you wore. What you drank, what you ate, and what you left on your dinner plate. I can remember how you smelled. I can picture how your eyes sought me. How you waited for the music to change. Our first dance, *"L'amour Existe Encore"* how you whispered the words in my ear, the ear with the missing earlobe, the one you didn't pull back from when you felt its deformity."

I revisited the kiss and the sense of falling into him. "I fell, Rahul, I fell into you and haven't been able to climb out. Don't leave me. I don't know how to climb out. I don't want to climb out."

Then I kissed him, willing him to kiss me, hoping it would wake him up. The sharpness of the missed opportunity made me gasp and I held my stomach.

I watched for any sign that my kiss had caused a reaction. I search for something, anything to give me hope.

Nothing. Rahul was unresponsive.

Hot tears multiplied and big drops fell unhindered onto his face. The stillness persisted. The pain in my heart became unbearable. My body froze, my lungs stopped working, the noise from the machines silenced and grew like a deep dark void. *Am I destined to have my heart ripped out of me? Will it stop this time?*

"Don't leave me, not after we've found each other. Not now. I won't survive. I don't want to survive. Not if you are not with me." I slumped down on the chair.

* * *

I DIDN'T KNOW how long my head rested on the bed. I imagined him slipping away, not wanting to come back to me.

Something skittered in my heart and woke me up with a start, but Rahul was still as a statue. I climbed onto the bed and lay down next to him, helpless and exhausted. I took his hand and held it gently in mine. My eyes closed and I fell asleep.

I felt the slightest squeeze around my fingers. Groggy from my disturbed sleep, I ignored it, but when I felt it again, I leapt off the bed and stared at his face. The night light cast it into shadow.

"Hema." His voice was raspy. He said my name again. His eyelids fluttered.

He was awake. Rahul was awake.

The tightness around my chest loosened.

"Hema."

I held the sippy cup of water to his mouth.

He took a few sips and a grimace twitched on his face. "I heard you. I heard you, my dil. You brought me back."

‹THIRTY FIVE›

OCTOBER ARRIVED. The winds grew bitter, the weather chilled. I had moved permanently into the house in Richmond and stopped the pretence of living with Mini. Amelie needed me near her, and I needed the Raichuras. Ma and I had grown closer, much closer through our time in hospital. I learnt more about Rahul's father. Ma spoke of how she had struggled at the loss of her husband and how Sharmila, her best friend, and Mukesh, had taken care of Rahul and Hasmita.

One day we were in the canteen at the hospital while Rahul had his wounds redressed. Ma spoke of her job at the building society, how she had worked her way up to assistant branch manager. We sipped our tea.

"I stopped working after Rahul's stay in hospital." A tear rolled down her cheek. "That was my *annus horribilis;* isn't that what the Queen said, the year Princess Diana and Prince Charles's marriage broke down?"

I nodded.

"That year Sharmila became ill too. Poor Mukesh, he did a lot of travelling from Wales to France." She blew her nose and sat with her head lowered. She didn't speak until our cups had emptied, the rawness of the hurt visible in her sad eyes. "Sharmila had breast cancer; it had spread by the time she told Mukesh. They say doctors are the last to notice health issues in their family."

We sat in quiet contemplation for a long time, Gayatri thinking of her best friend while I wondered what my life would have been like if I hadn't seen the advert. I felt honoured to have found a mother who was so kind-hearted and loyal.

***

ONE NIGHT I woke with a pang of overwhelming guilt. The tablets to help me sleep had long gone, and Rajni in flames filled my dreams. Images of her clutching at Rahul, his arms thrashing at her, trying to push her away. *Fire does that to people. No matter how you want to help, it is a powerful enemy that can devour you whole.*

I should have gone back into the room, I thought. *I should have helped her.*

A faint cry came from the room opposite. *"Papa,* please help me. I want *Papa."*

I roused myself from bed and made my way to Amelie's room. Ma sat with her already, her chest heaving.

"Can I sit with Amelie?"

The haunting eyes of the little girl focused on me. Her grandmother left the room.

"Hello, jinki dikri, did you have a nightmare?"

"I want *Papa;* can I go to *Papa?*"

I pushed the tendrils of hair that clung to her forehead away. "Shush, shush, we'll go soon, I promise. Do you want me to sing to you?"

Her eyes flickered a yes, and I sang the song her father sang to her. The song from *Kabhi Kabhie* about a little angel came to the house.

Once she had fallen asleep, I went to the kitchen. Ma was at the stove, watching a pan of simmering hot milk infused with cardamom and saffron.

"I'm so glad you came into our life, Hema. My son is lucky to have found you. My family is blessed to have found so many people to help us. Without Mukesh and Sharmila, my children would not be who they are now. All I did was go to work and feed them. They were the ones who nurtured them. I wish Sharmila were here. I miss her; she would know what to do. I'm not as good as her. I find it hard." She lifted her cup, and the hot milk soothed us.

"Do you remember Mukesh coming to the house in France?" She turned her cup in the saucer. "He told me he wanted to marry me. We are grandparents, and there he was, talking of getting married. Rahul was all for it. He and Debjani thought it was a great idea." Her lips turned upwards and her face lifted.

Why is she was telling me this? I knew of the engagement. I'd been there when they'd announced it.

"I knew the year Mukesh and I mourned for the loss of Sharmila that our bond was deeper than friendship. But how could I betray my best friend, and my husband?" Her eyes moistened, and I rested my hand on hers to comfort her. She continued to explain how Bhoomi had struggled most with the loss of her mother – she was the daughter Ma worried about most – and how all the children had been supportive of their decision.

"When you came into our life, I knew we'd found someone special. I knew that you'd make Rahul happy. It wasn't your fault, you rescued Rahul, you saved us. My son knew he loved you the moment he met you, just like he knew that Mukesh and I would be together eventually. Poor Rajni struggled with her demons, but he never held her in his heart. You must hold onto that Hema. Hold onto the fact that he holds you in his heart."

"SEE, SEE what I did for you, *Papa.*" Amelie came running into Rahul's hospital room and skipped into his lap. He winced, but the sparkling grin returned instantly.

She lifted a card with a drawing of a family on the front. "It's us, it's our family." She explained who everyone was in the picture. There was a row of couples, each with their names above. The children sat in front of the parents, each one holding a name card. For a five-year-old, the drawing was remarkable.

Rahul couldn't stop kissing Amelie's head as she pointed to everyone. Her adoring gaze drifted to his face for approval. The grin that had started when she burst into the room gleamed from ear to ear. The anxiety of her first visit to hospital to see her father seeped out of me and I leant on the bed. Her grandmother took my hand, and the dimple appeared on her cheek at last.

"She's been working on that for days," she whispered. "Isn't it lovely to see her talk so much?"

Rahul pulled the drawing for a closer look. "Why have I got a beard?"

Amelie replied, "*Mémé* said you were asleep. How can you shave when you're sleeping?"

He ran his fingers across his jaw. "You're right, but a glowing ray of light gave me a shave in my sleep." He winked at me, his eyes twinkling from the joy of seeing Amelie. The morning after his waking, she'd been the first person he'd asked for, and as Rahul had slept less and sat more upright, he'd asked to have his daughter brought to him.

"Now eat this." She skipped off his lap and rummaged through her grandmother's bag. "I made gajjar no halwo. *Mémé* let me grate the carrots and I stirred and stirred until my arm ached."

"My favourite, *ma pitchounette*. How did you know?" He ate the sweet with gusto, smacking his lips. Our little girl grew taller and brighter as she saw that her *papa* was better.

She stayed until seven o'clock that evening, but before leaving, she asked him to sing the song he always sang to her. The song that she would put on her music player every time she thought of him.

His voice, a deep baritone, echoed over the machines. "Mere ghar aayi…"

Amelie sat on his lap, her thumb in her mouth, and Ma dabbed at her cheeks from the pleasure of seeing her granddaughter happy.

When Amelie and Ma left, Rahul asked me what had happened the night Rajni had died. I had to tell him what I had done, how I'd left her in the room. How the paramedics had found a pulse, but she had died en route to the hospital.

He cried long, hard tears for her. I held onto the guilt for making him sad again.

I left early that day, unable to watch him cry, unable to shake the remorse, and broke down to Ma. I spoke of being responsible for Amelie's nightmares and Rahul's sadness. The memory of my many stays in hospital had taken up so much space in my head recently. I had to tell her about my accident. The number of operations because of the contractures on my arm and neck. How the skin needed many incisions. The days of my childhood, of the bullying at junior school. My time locked up in a cupboard and why I stayed away from my family home.

She held me as I cried and I told her I couldn't bear to watch Rahul go through the procedures anymore. Eventually, my heart quieted and as she stood at the door to leave my bedroom, she told me she was proud of how well I'd coped with my life after the accident. She told me I didn't have to take on the burden of looking after Rahul on my own, that she was there to help too.

THIRTY SIX

MINI AND I were in the bedroom. She and Dennis had come in the morning for Durga puja and for Navratri ni aadham. Ma always performed the aarti at the festival. But this year was the first Durga puja for her as the female head of the Biswas family.

In the morning, we had dressed Amelie as the living incarnation of Durga, in a red saree and gold jewellery with a small golden crown on her head. She had grinned and laughed throughout the ceremony as everyone told her she was the divine goddess.

After a delicious dinner of Bengali and Gujarati dishes, we all prepared to get dressed for the garba night. Mini was ready and watching as I pleated the grass-green silk saree, one of many given to me by the Raichuras, each with a short blouse, low-cut at the back. I had never worn saree blouses that revealed my scars before and my instincts told me to drape it to cover my back and arm.

I took in a deep breath. Not only would my scars be visible, but everyone would see my hands too, the palms still red from the burns.

"Wear it Gujarati-style; the pallu is beautiful," Mini urged as she sat on the bed.

"I can't," I said, and draped the pallu over my left shoulder.

"Why not?" Rahul leant against the door frame with his arms crossed.

"People will stare," I replied. He had gone into our bathroom to change into a long ultramarine jabo with cream churidar. A cream silk scarf draped over his shoulder. He came into the room and pulled at the saree's end.

Mini hurried to the door. "I'll see you downstairs."

His eyes drifted down to the tips of my toes as he stood behind me and stared at my reflection in the mirror. A shudder ran down my body. He loosened the pleats and pulled the pallu over my right shoulder.

"I want you to show your beautiful skin. It is exquisite." He took the end and tucked it into my waist.

I gulped in some much-needed air as he planted soft kisses on my exposed back. I leant into him, unable to resist. He pulled back my hair and nibbled at my ear. My heart quickened. I turned, and, as our lips met, his tongue explored my mouth.

I was lost, free-falling, my heart pounding.

* * *

AMELIE AND HER grandmother were waiting at the bottom of the stairs, both dressed in fuchsia pink, Ma in a saree and Amelie in a matching chaniya choli.

We had gone to garba last year when I lived at the house, and most of Ma's wardrobe was dark with the somber shades that widows wore, but after the engagement, she had introduced some brighter colours. That evening she had a small vermillion dot on her forehead too.

As we entered the incense-infused hall, some people greeted us as usual, but others whispered behind their hands as they saw the red vermillion tilak on Ma's forehead. Mukesh and Rahul hovered by her as she spoke with the brahmin who was preparing the shrine.

Not everyone in the Hindu community approved of widows getting married again, but the man smiled at the couple.

Rahul gestured to me to join them. Ma patted a space next to her, and I sat cross-legged in front of the picture of Ambe Maa.

"Ramesh Bhai, this is my vahu, Hema, Rahul's future wife."

The brahmin told Rahul to sit down next to me. Amelie sat by her grandmother. The priest put a vermillion dot on our foreheads and blessed us. We stood up, beckoned the rest of family and the musicians sang, "Jai adhya shakti, maa jai adhya shakti."

As we joined in chanting the aarti, Amelie grabbed the edge of the aarti plate and slid between Rahul and me. Rahul's faced beamed as he looked down at his daughter, and he pulled me closer, his hand resting on my lower back.

* * *

ON THE SIXTEENTH of November, we drove to Cardiff and split into two groups. The bride's family stayed at the Raichuras' and the groom's family stayed at the Biswases'. Although Mukesh had moved into the house after the fire, he was still a resident of Cardiff, so the marriage was to take place there. We had arranged lunch and a short religious blessing at the local mandir. The community of Hindus who had helped both families cope with their loss were happy to celebrate their union.

We travelled to City Hall at 11 a.m. on Saturday the seventeenth of November, the day of Rahul's birthday. The couple stepped out onto the steps, Hasmita and Suresh behind them. A cloud of multicoloured confetti rose as the grandchildren hurled fistfuls. Omkar, Debjani's son, stepped forward with a camera, and everyone lined up for photographs.

Afterwards, we drove to the mandir. The bride and groom waited in the car as the community prepared to welcome them. Amelie was so excited she broke the line and ran in holding a flower basket.

"Get ready, they are coming," she shrilled as she ran back to the hall.

Hasmita hurriedly took her back. The girls threw flower petals on the floor as Gayatri and Mukesh walked in, the rest of their friends waiting to welcome them by the wall of deities. The granddaughters all wore forest-green chaniya choli. Joyti, Radhika and Urvi, Mukesh's three teenage granddaughters, ushered Maya and Amelie to the front. His grandsons, Jai and Aahan, lined up on either side of the couple, and Omkar followed carrying Devan.

As they stood in front of Radha Krishna, the eternal lovers, Rahul gave his mother a flower garland

and Debjani handed her father his. They exchanged the jaimala. Everyone clapped and exchanged hugs and kisses. The children distributed barfi and sondesh.

After a delicious Gujarati lunch, Hasmita, Bhoomi and the grandchildren disappeared. The sound system blared, "Hey kha na na," the song "Dholi Taro Dhol Bhaaje" from *Hum Dil De Chuke Sanam.*

The children ran in clapping; the boys wore sun-yellow kediyu with abla embroidery and royal blue dhoti, and the girls wore scarlet chaniya cholis with sun-yellow chundadi with abla embroidery. As the garbo progressed, Hasmita and Bhoomi pulled all the guests into the dance.

It was lovely to see Gayatri and Mukesh being accepted as a couple by their friends in the community. That evening, we cut a cake to celebrate Rahul's thirty-ninth birthday. It hadn't felt like a wedding, more like a blessing to celebrate that we had survived the fire.

My heart swelled as I celebrated in my good fortune of finding a family who had welcomed me with open arms.

THIRTY SEVEN

RAHUL WAS HOLDING a letter, dismay written on his face, as I brought in our mid-morning coffee.

I tugged it out of his clenched fist. The beautifully neat writing swam before my eyes. The words trapped the air in my lungs. My legs gave way from under me and I fell into the chair.

My dear Rahul,
I write this with a heavy heart. It is a secret I have kept with me, but you'll understand why I did it after you read this letter.
That night when you woke up passed out in Rajni's room, she hadn't spent the night with you. You were too drunk to have done anything. She was cross that you'd passed out and insisted we go dancing, so we left you. You know what it was like back then with Rajni, the disappearances and the loss of memories. She'd disappeared with some guy and had come home still inebriated and passed out next to you.
I tried, Rahul, believe me. I tried to stop her, to persuade her to reduce the drugs. I even reminded her of the stay in hospital. When she found out she was pregnant with Amelie, she got into a programme, stayed off the drugs, and then when Amelie was born, the old demons resurfaced, her paranoia worse than before. I really thought being a mother

would change her, but she was back to lying and stealing to help her habit. I'm not proud of what I did. I wrote a letter to your mother pretending to be Rajni. I lied to Gayatri and to you about Amelie. I was desperate to help her, I had my parents to look after, Rajni's money had ran out and I knew you still felt something for her.

You really did help her to recover, and she was getting better. At times, when I met her, she was back to the Rajni we knew and loved. The belle of Marseille. I bought the ticket for England for her and I persuaded Céleste to let her in that night. I am sorry that it resulted in her death and your injury. I was only trying to help my friend reunite with her child, nothing more. I am saddened that Amelie has lost her mother, but my guilt is gnawing at me. I must tell you Amelie is not your child. I don't know who her father is. Rajni didn't know and didn't care. She was always headstrong, did whatever she wanted and didn't think of the consequences or what the world thought. It was her way. I'm sorry, I should have told you before, but now that Rajni is gone, I thought you should know of Amelie's parentage.

I am and will always be your friend. Please forgive me, Madeleine.

The weight of his hand rested on my shoulder; the little ridges in his palm reminded me of that night again. I had to use all my strength to fight the angry tears that threatened to erupt.

"Why would she lie to you and Ma?"

He gently pulled me up, his expression wary.

"Does this mean the adoption is illegal?"

Rahul explained that, as he was Amelie's legal guardian, this news had changed nothing.

I pushed him away and paced back and forth, back and forth. My hands fisted. The enormity of what I had read seeped through to the pit of my stomach. "I can't lose her. They have never liked me. What should I do, what should I do?" I mumbled to myself. I'd seen the scorn on Céleste and Madeleine's face when Amelie clung to me.

He gripped my shoulders. "Stop, my dil." His arms held me, and I broke down and wept uncontrollable tears.

The fear turned to anger again, and I thrashed at him. "Madeleine knows, Rahul! She knows. How can you be so calm?"

I put as much distance between us as I could. *He doesn't care; he doesn't love Amelie. He was only looking after her because he thought she was his child.* "You don't care! Is that why you're not upset? What if Madeleine tells the father? What if he wants her?" Questions tumbled out of my mouth as all I'd learnt of Rahul's kindness slipped out of my mind. The fear of losing Amelie, my child, my little girl, overwhelmed any logic.

"Stop it! Stop being ridiculous. Madeleine only knows that it's not me!" he shouted, his eyes sharp as lead. "She doesn't know who it is, my dil. She would have written that in there!" He stabbed at the sheet that had fallen on the rug.

There was a quiet knock on the study door; Ma's head popped through. "What's wrong?"

"Come and sit down." Rahul picked up the letter and guided me to the seating area. As he explained the content of the note, his mother's body grew still. She held herself straight as an arrow, fingers entwined. Her gaze found mine and then her son's.

She inhaled a slow deep breath and said, "You'd better find a way to keep her, Rahul. I will not give up my granddaughter that easily. Silence Madeleine and Céleste, if you must. Rajni was—" She stopped mid-sentence. "—she is gone, poor child. She had a tough time. Seeing all that destruction."

* * *

RAJNI'S BODY was released a week later, after the inquest. Her act of betrayal of the people I loved gnawed at my soul. How could she hurt two of the kindest people who'd supported her, not only financially, but emotionally? What had she experienced to make her do that?

The quiet Hindu ceremony took place at the crematorium. Rahul, his parents, Amelie and I were the only ones present. Rahul had called Madeleine after the release and informed her of the date. He had declared that she was not welcome, and he did not want her to contact our daughter. He emphasised the word *daughter*, his voice vibrating with anger and hurt.

For lunch, instead of the usual chaas and rotla, we ate a meal of Rajni's favourite foods. She had suffered in her brief life, a life where she had witnessed the trauma of displacement and the death of her loved ones. But, even through adversity, she had held a short but successful career. She had created a being, the baby girl who was our daughter.

I vowed to tell Amelie of the successes of her mother's life, not the destruction and annihilation that had become her later life. The whole time, I endured the burden of my actions, reliving my instinct to create a barrier against the fire. I had watched enough fire safety videos during my childhood to know that closed doors saved lives.

* * *

THAT NIGHT in bed, the scene of Rajni's death besieged my memories. I tossed and turned, unable to move away from the guilt over depriving our daughter of her only parent. I knew of the yearning for my family, and I had been responsible for taking Amelie's from hers.

The bedside lamp flicked on and Rahul gazed at me, his head propped up by his arm. "What's wrong, my dil?"

I told him of my guilt and how it plagued my mind.

He pulled me to him. "You saved everyone, that day. I am still here because of you. Amelie is lucky to have a mother like you. You are as fierce as the fire that scorched you. I've seen you protect her, and you did it that night. You rescued her. You, my love, are blessed by flames and never regret it. It is what has given you the strength and the kindness you give everybody. Don't feel guilty. It was not your fault."

He enveloped me in his arms and switched off the lamp. My head rested on his broad chest and our hearts synchronised, and I heard his reassuring words as I dozed off to sleep.

"Amelie is lucky to have a mother like you."

Rajni's Favourite Foods

Guwar nu shaak
Gujarati-style cluster beans curry

Suku chana nu shaak
Steamed black chickpea flavoured with ginger, garlic and green chili

Methi na bhajia
Deep fried fenugreek leaves and gram flour fritters

'Tameta ni chutnee
Fresh tomatoes chutney made with chopped coriander and green chillies

Rotli
Unleavened, round flatbread roasted in a griddle pan

Jeera baath
Fried rice with cumin

Kadhi
Thick spicy broth made from gram flour and natural yoghurt

Garam Mohanthal
Freshly prepared gram flour, milk and sugar sweet infused with mace and cardamom usually set in squares, but this time left as a thick pudding

Phulli gathiya
Star-shaped gram flour fried noodles with carom seeds

‘THIRTY EIGHT

THE DATE FOR our wedding was set during the Christmas holiday. And on the day Hasmita and her family arrived from Canada, we celebrated my twenty-third birthday at the local Italian restaurant. The following morning, my cousins arrived to take me to Preston.

Knots formed in my stomach as we pulled off the M6. The brief drive to Beechwood Close, my childhood home, dragged. My relationship with my family was nothing like Debjani, Hasmita and Bhoomi's, who turned up at the drop of a hat to spend time with their parents, as they had last night. Mini poked her head to the back and smiled brightly as we pulled up onto the driveway.

"Chin up, H.P. You're home," Dennis urged.

My aunt came running to the front door, but instead of grabbing her favourite child, she drew me to her. I was ashamed of my thoughts. She had changed and had spoken to me every week since the fire. Her voice filled with concern as she asked after our well-being and of Amelie's progress in school.

It had been Mami, not Mama, who'd sat at my bedside and brought me distractions when all I'd wanted to do was stare at Rahul.

Kalpesh Mama beamed behind her. "My turn, Chanda; hug the other two," he said as he pulled me to him.

I loved coming home to Mama's hugs. The scent of his cologne unravelled the knots in my back.

My last days as Hema Pattni differed greatly from my early years in Preston. One afternoon, when we were sorting through my outfits for the various ceremonies, my aunt began a halting conversation.

"I am sorry, Hema, please forgive me." For the first time in my life, I saw copious tears roll down her cheeks. "I haven't been a loving mother to you. I wasn't good enough." The droplets slid down her neck. "I am not as brave and strong as you and Meena." She told me of her inability to be with me at the hospital when I was younger and how her vigils had grown infrequent. How as a child, I'd lashed out at her as she'd washed me and creamed me, then asked for her husband instead. How it had become difficult for her to care for me. Her instinct to protect me had turned to resentment as I'd lashed out at her.

"I regret my actions. I was too immature. Before you go to your sasara, I want you to know I am very proud of you. You have grown into a remarkable woman."

***

"COME ON, before she finds out we're missing." Mini held the blankets in her arms, and I pulled at the pillow and ran back into my bedroom, remembering someone very special.

"Where did you go?" Mini said, when I came back. She'd picked up the piles of old newspapers and put them in a heap in the corner. Her eyes focused on Peggy, cradled under my armpit.

We got to work spreading one of the blankets on the floor. I threw the pillow on top and sat the soft squidgy Cabbage Patch doll who went with me everywhere next to it. Mini popped out of the cupboard and came back in with the blanket neatly folded. She could do that on her own, but I needed help. My back and armpit hurt when I raised my arms too high. Kalpesh Mama said it would get better, that I needed to moisturise more, but it hurt, and Mami's hands weren't gentle. Her hands were like sharp claws, just like her words, piercing my back, bleeding my soul. When Mama used the ointment, his hands felt like feather strokes. It still burnt, but he was much gentler, his hands much softer.

"Come on Hema, let's get the food."

We sneaked into the dining room where a full spread of food had been laid out: crispy bhajia, samosa, katchori, khaman dokhla, a big bowl of mattar baath, two shaaks, one potato, the other ringda ne valor, kadhi and puri and glasses filled with fizzy drinks.

"Quick, before anyone sees us!" Mini filled her plate and grabbed a glass of Coke.

I did the same and picked up a lemonade.

That was the first time I ate in the cupboard under the stairs. I'd forgotten why we'd gone in there in the first place, forgotten that Mini was often with me keeping me company. I'd forgotten that when I was younger, my aunt had made my favourite food, khaman dokhla, for breakfast.

Now I picked up Peggy from the bookshelf and sat on the edge of bed. *When did I start resenting her? When did our relationship break down?*

***

"MEENAXI! Come out at once. No more eating in the den."

Chanda Mami was at the door, her face red, her beady eyes full of anger. She'd allowed us to sit in there with sweets and snacks while she was busy with keeping everyone entertained and filled with food. But it had changed when Mini had become ill and my aunt had stopped her from sneaking in and eating all the "bad sugary food", as she called it.

"Hide, Hema, go and get your stuff and stay there." Dennis held his arms splayed out as he prevented Hari and the others from hurting and tormenting me with their words and kicks.

Hari Patel, short, stout and acne-faced, had picked on me and often swung me around by my bad arm. How had I blanked that out? The pain of the memory knocked the air out of my stomach and I squeezed Peggy close to my chest.

Why had I forgotten Hari? Who was still short, stout and acne-faced. Who continued to sneer at me when we met, his small black eyes filled with contempt. A grown man who still lived with his parents, who had not ventured out of Preston.

All the memories of conversations I'd neglected to remember came back.

"Leave her alone, Mummy, she likes to be in there when everyone comes. It helps her." Dennis' muffled voice came through the cupboard door.

"What will people say? That I hide her away, that I'm ashamed? She brings so much trouble, that girl. I'll have to tell them something."

"Tell them she's shy, tell them she is in hospital. No one will know she's inside the cupboard."

She'd stopped tapping at the door. A few minutes later, I heard the three taps, a pause, tap and repeat. Dennis had a secret code to be allowed in.

His head popped through the door. "She's gone. I'll bring you some food when it's put out."

***

I THOUGHT of all the happy times my cousins and I had spent in the cupboard under the stairs. How we'd squeezed in for secret snacks, the little hoard that Dennis had built over the week, stealing biscuits and sweets from the cupboard. The memories brought a smile to my face.

Chanda Mami's brows met. "What are you thinking about?"

"Did you know we had a secret stash of biscuits and snacks in the cupboard under the stairs?"

Her round face lit up and a smile grew from ear to ear. "Of course I did, nothing escapes me. Who do you think kept it tidy? You know how much I hate mice."

I squeezed her hands to stop them shaking at the mention of mice.

She continued. "You were so independent, you collected your own cereal bowl, adding just enough milk to soak the cornflakes. I suppose staying in hospital so many times does that to children. I could never do any good with you. Even when it came to breakfast, you insisted on cereal during the weekday. 'Just like mama' you'd say, 'proper breakfast on weekends.' When you were younger, you followed him everywhere. In fact, I'm surprised that Meena is becoming a doctor. I thought you'd follow in your mama's footsteps."

I pulled her fingers apart. "It's okay, I understand." It was in that moment I realised why I had behaved the way I did. I'd blamed her for the pain she'd inflicted and had made her life difficult. I looked back at all my minor acts of defiance. I'd had the urge to hit back at the injustice of losing my family.

All the advice from my support group finally made sense. The talking with Gayatri of how my relationship with my aunt could be salvaged made sense. I needed to let go of the guilt. The guilt of being the only survivor. I had made it my reason to rebel, and guilt had become my only emotion. It was time I let it go.

"I wouldn't know how to cook, clean and be self-reliant if you hadn't done what you did," I reassured her, trying to keep my voice light, holding back the overwhelming desire to cry.

"But daughters aren't supposed to be self-supporting, Hema. Their families take care of them."

I pulled her into a hug, my eyes watering. "Not in this age, Mami. Women don't need looking after." I sobbed into her shoulder.

THIRTY NINE

FRIDAY LUNCH was spent in the marquee set up in the garden. Rahul and his family had arrived that morning and had checked into their hotel. The ladies from the mandir had prepared a feast with three shaaks, kadhi, baath, with the usual accompaniments for a celebratory Gujarati meal.

Afterwards, the women and girls gathered in the huge tent for the applying of mehndi on their hands. Wedding songs played on a sound system set up by Dennis.

I asked for decoration on my palms and the sides of my feet. My complexion was too dark to show the intricate lacy patterns of the henna paste.

Rahul's sisters sat around me, insisting that I had the backs painted too. "Don't forget to hide Rahul's initials in there," Mami instructed as she carried in a tray of soft drinks, then pulled his siblings away.

Puja, the lady who'd come to decorate our hands with henna, had brought a friend along, and she was drawing a flowery design on the back of Mini's hands. Amelie sat next to me, her hands held aloft, waiting patiently for the mehndi to dry. By three o'clock, the duo who'd applied the henna were preparing to leave. Ma fetched Rahul into the tent and asked for a pattern on her son's hand too. He winked at me and whispered something in Puja's ears, and she blushed at him.

After chai and nasto of khaman dhokla, the Raichuras prepared to go back to their hotel to dress for the joint Sanji. As everyone was piling into their cars, Rahul pulled me into the marquee. His warm palms radiated a tingle on my exposed waist.

"I've hated waking up without you. Did you miss me, my dil?"

I glanced at my painted hands and lifted my forearms to rest on his shoulders. "Kiss me. You haven't kissed me," I said, and our lips touched as the entire length of our bodies aligned. Our hearts recognised each other, and the beats synchronised.

"Let go of him, H.P.," Dennis chortled. "Gayatri Masi and Mukesh Masa are waiting for the groom."

Rahul led me down the hallway and planted a lingering kiss on my lips in front of everyone. The heat of embarrassment rose to my cheeks.

Hema and Rahul's Mehndi Lunch

Ringda ne mattar ñu shaak
Aubergine and peas curry

Tindoora ñu shaak
Ivy gourd curry

Chuti mug ni dall
lightly steamed split mung bean lentil cooked with mild spices

Bateta ni kadhi
thick spicy broth made from gram flour and natural yoghurt and diced potatoes

Navratan Baath
Fried rice with carrots, sweetcorn, peas and potatoes

Puri
Fried round flatbread made with whole wheat flour

Kheer
Rice pudding infused with saffron

Bateta Vada
Fried spicy mashed potato balls coated with gram flour batter

Kachumber
A salad made with cabbage, cucumber, carrots, onions and tomatoes

Cobi gajjar no sambharo
Gujarati-style stir-fried cabbage, carrot and green chillies

Ambli khajjur ni chutnee
Tamarind date chutney

Far far and Papad
Fried tapioca or rice flour crisps and thinly lentil bread

* * *

I WAITED PATIENTLY in front of my dressing table to get dressed for the evening. My long locks were set in curls, two strands pushed from my face by clips, teardrop pendants hung over my ears. My non-existent ear prevented me from wearing the earrings, but the jeweller had created these specially for me. A matching tika rested on my forehead.

My bedroom door opened, and I turned my head. Mami held her hands to her heart and beamed affectionately. Mini followed behind her with my outfit in her arms. The garment, made of embroidered silk in parrot green, glistened in the light.

"Let's get you ready." Mini held up the choli, a long top, its back covered in a net that matched my skin tone. Rows of eyelets ran down the narrow sides, creating the effect of a corset. The sleeves were a three-quarters length.

"Put a black mark behind Hema's ear, nazar lage jase."

"Mummy, that's rubbish," Mini said.

"But I believe it." She kissed me on the head. "Hema is stunning today, and she needs no more rotten luck."

* * *

AS THE CAR pulled up in front of the Gujarati Hindu Society Centre, Rahul ran to open the door. He was wearing a long primrose silk jabo embroidered in gold with a dark vermillion waistcoat and baggy matching pyjamas.

"My dil, you take my breath away." His lips brushed the back of my hand, and we waited outside Gita Hall, the entrance adorned with red, orange and green swags for the Sanji night. The band played "Saajan ke ghar jaana" from *Lajja*. As Rahul and I entered to the cheer of the waiting crowd, Amelie ran towards us and pushed herself in between, grabbing our hands.

The musical group sang wedding songs as we ate our evening meal of vegetarian party food. After dinner, we sat expectantly on the chairs placed around the sides of the room for a dance performance.

I turned to Rahul as he slowly lifted a brow and winked, his eyes twinkling. The new Rahul, the smiling, teasing one, was different, and his family beamed at him as much I did. The burden and remorse he had held for Rajni's illness had slowly left him as he'd watched Amelie blossom into a happy child. The nightmares had eased and even she seemed lighter and brighter after the death of her mother.

The band played a familiar tune; Rahul posed in the middle of the room, the children positioning themselves in a line behind him. The male singer sang, and Rahul and the youngsters danced to "Mehndi laga ke rakhna, doli saja ke rakhna" from *Dilwale Dulhania Le Jayenge*. By the end of the song, they encouraged everyone onto the dance floor, even the old ladies, who hardly danced.

As the evening progressed, Rahul and I twirled and danced the dandiya raas, our daughter by our side. After teas and coffee, the band announced one more dance. Rahul guided me to wait by the entrance.

One of the girls thrust a toy guitar into my hand as Rahul stood at the mic.

"Friends, family, this song is very important to Amelie and me. If we hadn't found Hema, we wouldn't be the happiest people in the whole world."

Amelie nodded vehemently as Rahul held out his hand to her. "'Koi mil gaya.' I found someone, we found someone very special. My wife."

He pointed the mic to Amelie, who said, "My *maman*."

We performed the dance that had brought us together. The first time, I'd known I'd found a place in my heart for a sweet little girl and my one and only love.

Rahul remained by my side as we bid everybody goodnight. I wanted to kiss him but felt awkward about doing so in front of all the people. His smouldering eyes never left mine.

Hema and Rahul's Sanji

Bombay sandwich
Toasted sandwich made with tomatoes, cheese, onions, boiled potatoes and coriander chutney and special spice blend

Vegetable samosa
Deep fried triangular wheat pastry filled with potatoes, peas and carrots

Dahi vada
Ground lentils, fried dumplings, soaked in natural yogurt served with date and tamarind chutney

Pau Bhaji
Fried bread rolls with mashed spiced vegetable, and butter served with diced onions

Bhel
Crispy gram flour, thin noodles and puffed rice with boiled chickpeas and potatoes served with three types of chutney: date and tamarind, green chilli and coriander and garlic and red chilli, sprinkled with black salt and roasted cumin powder

Kitchi
Steamed rice flour dumplings served with flavoured oil, sesame, chilli or garlic

Boondi jamboo
Gram flour fried beads with mini milk and plain flour fried balls soaked in saffron-infused sugar syrup

Dhudhi no halwo
Bottle gourd cooked with thickened cream and sugar and cardamom

Malia, Badam, Keri ne Pista Kulfi
Assorted frozen dairy dessert infused with cardamom. cream, almond, mango and pistachio

FORTY

BY NINE THIRTY, we were home, and the Raichuras back in their hotel. As I prepared to go to bed, a tapping sound came from my window, then again.

Outside, Rahul waved at me. "Come down."

I ran quietly down the stairs and opened the kitchen door. "What are you doing here?"

"I didn't get my goodnight kiss, my dil," he whispered, and stepped inside the house.

A shiver raced down to my toes as our lips met. Our quickened breaths matched as we savoured each other's mouths, his hand exploring my back. The heat from it burnt my body. We were about to be married, and we were secretly making out like teenagers in an unlit kitchen. I should have insisted on staying at the hotel. A giggle rose in my throat.

"What?" He pulled away.

I held onto him, my head resting on his chest. I knew that if I looked up, his mischievous grin would result in my full belly laugh.

We heard a cough. Rahul's chin lifted off my head.

"What are you doing here?" Mama asked. I turned sheepishly towards him. Rahul's grip tightened.

"I wanted to… to tell Hema I was looking forward to seeing her under the mandap," he replied, sounding like a child who'd been caught misbehaving.

"In the dark? In my kitchen?" Mama walked to the front door and opened it. "I'll see you at ten thirty, Rahul, no earlier; no sneaking here to meet my daughter." His face was stern.

Rahul kissed my knuckles and then pulled my mouth to his, heating my body with a blush. He stepped out and grinned at my uncle. "I'll be there ten thirty sharp, sir."

"Really, Rahul, you have no shame." The panelled door closed on him.

I tried my hardest to push back the blush that had risen to my cheeks, keeping my eyes locked on the floor.

Mama put his arm around my shoulder. "Sometimes you have to make the groom uncomfortable." His lips lifted, and he said, "Go to bed, Hema, big day tomorrow."

I kissed him on the cheek and ran up to my room.

***

"WAKE UP, WAKE UP," Chanda Mami shrieked.

The time on the clock was 5.30 a.m. I pulled on my gown, grabbed my wash bag and waited outside the main bathroom. All night I'd dreamt of Rahul, his body against mine, our limbs entwined.

The idea of staying apart before the wedding was frustrating. My family and his knew we slept with each other. Why the pretence? But my mami had insisted that this was how it was going to be, the bride leaving from her parents' home and the groom arriving from his.

Mini yawned behind me. "Hurry up, Dennis. You're not first on the list." She pounded on the door.

It reminded me of childhood, Dennis hogging the family bathroom, Mini banging the door, and me mastering the art of napping while standing.

Mini pulled at my shoulders and turned me towards my room. "Go back to sleep; I'll fetch you."

"My bathroom's free, girls!" Kalpesh Mama pointed as he stepped out of his bedroom, dressed in a dove-grey sherwani.

"Can't, my wash bag is in there." She stabbed at the door.

I took my towel from the airing cupboard.

When I came downstairs, Dennis was chomping toast like only he could. He was dressed in a pale turquoise sherwani with cream churidar, his matching scarf over the dining chair. Chanda Mami was fussing over her favourite child, buttering his toast, filling a bowl of fruit. Although she'd showered, she was wearing a dressing gown, her long hair in curlers. I had put on a pair of harem pants and a T-shirt. Chanda Mami placed a bowl of chopped fruit and a plate of farali chevdo, barfi and badam nu dhudh in front of me. The phone rang and Mini came running down the stairs to pick it up. She was also dressed in slouchy clothes like mine; Prafula, who was doing our hair and makeup, would also dress us for the wedding.

"Hems! It's for you."

I grabbed the handset from her.

"Good morning, my dil. I have a present for you; ask Mini to give it to you. Don't open it in front of anyone. It's private. Before I let you go, I have someone else here who wants to speak with you."

"*Maman,* are you excited? I dreamt of Disneyland. When did you say we were going?"

Amelie's excited voice sent a swathe of happiness through me. Rahul had booked a trip to America straight after we came back from our honeymoon, for the three of us.

We would finally be a family, Rahul, Amelie and me.

***

THE SMALL SQUARE box that sat on the bedside table crept into my vision intermittently while my hair was teased and styled into a low bun. Mini walked in with my panetar, a pure-white silk saree with a bright crimson border. The saree blouse was red and the sleeves rested above my elbow, the back low, revealing my scars.

"I have something for you." Mama entered the room, followed by Mami, who wore a forest-green and gold silk saree, her hair put up in an elaborate hairstyle.

He approached slowly, his hands behind his back, and revealed a dark-red velvet jewellery box. Inside it were a gold necklace, a ring, two tear-shaped brooches that matched the pendant on the necklace, a tear-shaped tika and four matching kada.

"The set belonged to your mother. We had the earrings made into brooches."

"I asked the jeweller to make a matching tika," Mami added.

Mini opened the clasp on the necklace and Prafula used the converted earrings to pin up my pallu. My mami held up my wrists and filled them with red bangles, the ornate kada on either side. Once the tika was placed in the centre of my forehead, my aunt and uncle kissed me and left the room.

"I'll leave you to open that." Mini pointed to the package, sniffing as she grabbed my small overnight suitcase.

My heart soared like a bird, unable to stay in its place. I had never imagined that I'd be marrying Rahul. The man I'd met in a dream, the man who had fallen in love with me, despite my scars, despite the age difference. After the ceremony I would be spending the rest of my life with the two people who had stolen my heart that summer in Aix.

I inhaled and opened the gift-wrapped parcel. There was a cream silk garter with blue ribbons folded inside; wedged to the lid was a slim, ornate card. As I lifted the ribbon, a gold chain with a flame-shaped pendant encrusted with diamonds slipped out. I picked up the gold strand and read the note.

My dil,
The flame signifies that we were meant to be together.
When I met you that night, you were like a divo burning in the temple. Like a glowing ray of light.
Flames blessed you. Fire blessed me, and later today, Agni Dev will bless us under the mandap. I can't wait to spend the rest of my life with you.
My love for you is made in heaven.
Your Rahul.

I clipped the necklace around my neck, pulled up my saree and slipped the garter on my left thigh, thinking how thoughtful it was of Rahul to get me something blue. I already had something old, my mother's set; something new, my panetar; something borrowed, Mini's gold hairclips; and, as the Lancashire tradition went, my mami had brought two old silver sixpences, put them in a red velvet pouch and attached it to the kandoro on my waist.

"Ready? Come on everyone, time to go!" Chanda Mami yelled.

I took a deep breath and one final look at myself in the mirror before leaving my childhood bedroom.

My family watched at the bottom of the stairs. Dennis held his hand to his heart and my mama pulled his wife to his side, his eyes glistening. Chanda Mami raised her hands and pressed her knuckles to her head. Huge globes of tears welled in Mini's eyes.

I pulled my sister to me and scolded her for being such a wimp. Mini had burst into tears so frequently these last few days we'd all been taken by surprise, wondering what had changed in the strong independent woman we'd loved.

Dennis handed her a tissue. "Dread to think what she's going to be like when it's her turn."

My mami blanched, but only for a fraction of time, and she smiled lovingly at her daughter.

FORTY ONE

MY FAMILY GATHERED to escort me to the mandap. Rahul's sisters had come with my dark vermillion garchoru, which partially covered my head and most of my back. Amelie and Maya were poised with baskets of flower petals to throw on our route.

I sat on the armchair placed at the entrance, and, as was the custom, my maternal uncle and my cousin lifted the seat and carried me to the canopy. The sound system played "Ek ladki ko dekha to aisa lega." Rahul had swapped the song we'd selected. The lyrics – 'when I saw this girl, she seemed to me like a blooming rose,' matched the words in the note. *Like a divo in the temple, like a glowing ray of light.*

The chair lowered and I stepped under the mandap. The antarpaat that had shielded my arrival dropped, and Rahul grinned at me. The occasional smiles that hollowed my legs were no longer rare, but spread easily on his face. He wore a cream brocade silk sherwani with a crimson red churidar and a pale-pink and crimson tie-dyed scarf on his shoulder.

Our eyes locked and Amelie nudged her *papa* and said, "Isn't *Maman* beautiful?"

He pulled her to his side. "She is that, *ma pitchounette*. She is a like a rose created just for us."

The Hindu wedding ceremony started with the jaimala, the exchange of flower garlands, an acceptance of the bride and groom of each other, a ritual performed since Vedic times. I would have been happy with just that, like Gayatri and Mukesh's wedding, but Rahul and my family had insisted we had the traditional Hindu ceremony, including the sacred rituals that called on all present to witness the marriage of the couple and the joining of the two families.

During the kanya daan, the part where the bride's parents hand their daughter to the bridegroom, tracks of tears rolled down Kalpesh Mama and Chanda Mami's cheeks. Rahul's family reassured them. Ma took my mami's hand and squeezed it.

A lump formed in my throat. The photographs of my parents and grandparents, displayed on the post of the mandap, smudged.

At the hastamelap, all the daughters tied the cheda chedi, Hasmita, Debjani and Bhoomi.

At the mangalphera, Rahul whispered, "At last, our blessing from Agni Dev," as we walked with our fingers entwined around the sacred fire, each round blessed by Dennis.

We took the seven vows of the septapadi, that we would look after each other and support each other in our duties to our families. Finally, Rahul lifted my ornamental tika and drew a line of sindoor in my parting and leant in, brushing his lips on my neck as he put on the mangalsutra, the sacred thread to signify that I was a married woman.

The vidaai was upsetting for both families. Mine were tearful to see me leave them, and Rahul's shed tears at the memory of how this day might not have come.

* * *

THE HUGE FOUR-POSTER bed rested against a dark wood-panelled wall, its posts draped with floral curtains. Garlands of maroon and cream roses crisscrossed the canopy. Rose petals were strewn across the bedsheet.

The lyrics of our song filled the luxurious room, "Kabhi kabhie mere dil me..." Sometimes, in my heart, a feeling emerges that you'll love me forever like this.

Rahul had undressed quickly and lay on the bed, his hands cupped behind his head. "Go on then, take off your clothes."

I pulled at my pleats slowly, pulling off one set, then another. His mouth fell open, his tongue licking his bottom lip.

My breath caught at the sight of the scars on his well-defined chest and arms, still red in places. His boxer shorts were unable to disguise his desire.

I loosened my hairstyle and slipped out of the bundle of cloth that rested on the floor. The bells on my ankles jingled.

"Don't take those off." He pointed to my anklets. He bit his lower lip, lust visible in his dark brown eyes.

I walked over to the side of the four-poster bed and turned. His touch made me shudder as he unfastened my blouse.

"Can't wait," he groaned, and his hungry mouth found mine as he pulled my remaining garments off. I was naked except for the garter and the ankle bracelets.

"Find your name first," he said.

He moaned as he lifted me onto the mattress and presented his right hand. I searched for my name in the circular patterns and traced it with my fingers; his eyelids closed fractionally at the touch of my fingertip.

So that was what he'd been whispering to Puja on our mehndi night. Usually, it was the groom who searched the bride's hand, but instead, he'd had my name painted on his palm.

He grabbed my hands and stared at the intricate design on my palm. "I. Give. Up." His words were throaty groans, and he flipped me on my back.

The bells jingled on my anklets. That night, the night of our wedding, the little chimes created music to accompany the cries that escaped our lips. The day I was finally his.

Tiny bells awoke me from my blissful sleep and I lifted the sheets as Rahul's fingers jingled my anklets.

"These… you have to wear these all the time." He slowly crawled up to me. "Good morning, my dil."

I kissed his luscious lips, and he reluctantly drew away.

"You know our song 'Kabhi Kabhie.'"

I pecked his lips again.

"It's about us – 'sometimes, in my heart, a feeling emerges, that you were created for me. That you were living among the stars, waiting for me to call you to come down to earth just for me.'" He whispered the words like a prayer.

"Think about it," he continued. "If your parents hadn't died, you probably wouldn't have taken the au pair job. If Rajni hadn't become ill, I wouldn't have had any need for you. I'm certain I'm not suitable husband material. The music we made last night, it is because our love is made in heaven. The symphony of Hema and Rahul." He chuckled.

"Come, Mrs Raichura." He paused. "How about we create another symphony in the shower?"

He effortlessly lifted himself off the petal-strewn bed and carried me fireman-style into the bathroom. I shook my legs teasingly and the bells jingled.

EPILOGUE

Summer 2006

"*MAMAN*, I'm going with *Papa* to pick up Nana and Nani," Amelie yelled as she raced towards the double garage.

I was in the kitchen, preparing lunch for Kalpesh Mama and Chanda Mami. I shook my head from side to side at the contrast in my relationship with them since my marriage. Mostly because of Rahul and his mother. When we were home in England, we saw them at least once a month.

The summer holidays were different. I had been running a language school in the South of France since 2002. After hearing of my inheritance, I'd quit my career in banking. What was the point? Being Mrs Rahul Raichura meant I was free to work, or not. But I could not give up the joy of teaching languages. My first year of school was just like my first summer in Aix. I provided language classes to teenagers and adults who required practice in English, German, Spanish, all the European languages. As I built up my linguistic skills, I included Mandarin, Polish and

Russian. The school grew through reputation, and we provided learning breaks with host families in all the European countries. Summer was the busiest season for us, and I usually employed an au pair and a housekeeper. Hélène Graux was also part of the team, managing the administration of the school from Aix-en-Provence.

I heard the squeals of our twins, Diya and Prem, who were playing in the garden with Sarah, a daughter of my accountant who wanted to strengthen her French. The twins had completed our family and their father doted on them as much as he did our daughter, the child that had brought us together. The squeals became louder and I decided to check what the commotion was about.

"Guess what?" My husband was leaning against the door; my heart lurched to my stomach, and my legs weakened as I caught sight of him. Even after all this time, his beaming face and sparkling eyes hitched my breath. I wiped my hands on the towel and walked up to him.

"What?" I frowned, straining to overhear any conversation on the terrace.

Rahul was back from picking up my parents. I was proud that my uncle and aunt regarded me as their offspring. I'd spoken at length to both Chanda Mami and Ma about how I felt, and Ma had advised.

"Sometimes, you must let go of your past to embrace your present."

So that was exactly what we'd both done. Let go of what had happened and started afresh, building a new life filled with new memories.

"I met someone else at the airport," Rahul said.

He pulled me to the patio. Sitting at the table were my family, Kalpesh Mama and Chanda Mami, Mini and Niraj, Dennis and Shreya. I stopped short, unable to take in the sight. My vision blurred as I sucked in a lungful of air. My grip tightened on Rahul's arm.

For the past four years, I'd badgered them to come to France, and, each time, they'd declined. That year, I'd started earlier than usual, giving them ample notice to adjust their holiday, and yet again they had refused.

Kalpesh Mama stood up, his arms spread. "No hugs for your dear old mama?"

I let go of Rahul and raised my arms around my mama's neck, resting my head on his shoulder. His familiar scent engulfed me. My heart swelled in my chest.

"*Papa* made us keep it a secret." Amelie herded the children to the patio with Sarah, who was holding a baby.

Mini and I still had our phone calls that lasted hours, even though she kept down a busy job at Charing Cross Hospital, had a two-year-old daughter, and had a husband who travelled to and from New York. But the major change was my relationship with Chanda Mami. She had come to visit as often as she could when the twins were born. She rang Rahul's mother at every turn to ask about us. Rahul and Dennis played golf together, so I met up with Shreya and the baby weekly. Dennis and Shreya had found each other two years ago, while they were both on a work ski trip. They'd instantly decided on getting married, to the annoyance of their families. The baby was their first child, a little boy who'd had his dadi and fiabas wrapped around his little finger within minutes of being born.

"Nani! Nani!" the twins shouted in unison and grabbed Chanda Mami.

She clucked. "Mara bachulyia, I've missed you."

Binita, Mini's daughter, pulled out of Amelie's grip and waddled over to Rahul, waving her chubby arms in the air.

He scooped her up, drew Amelie to his side, laughed and said, "So, *ma pitchounette,* best summer ever?"

"No, *Papa,* not yet. When will everybody else come?" And she clamped her hands over her mouth, looking shamefacedly at her father.

I couldn't suppress my grin at Rahul as I lifted the baby out of Sarah's arms. "How many more people have you asked to join us for the summer?"

"Only our nearest and dearest, my dil, only our nearest and dearest." He kissed our eldest child on her forehead. "You can't keep anything secret from your *maman,* can you?"

Everyone laughed. We were finally having a big family holiday, with the extended Biswas, Raichura and Jogia families celebrating Amelie Amin-Raichura's tenth birthday in France.

The country where I found my love.

THE END

GLOSSARY

Gujarati words

Aarti – a worship ritual with the lit flame known as a divo

Abla – traditional embroidery work using round mirrors and silk thread from Gujarat

Agni Dev – God of fire

Ajeeb aadmi hey who – what a strange man he is

Ambe Maa – also known as Durga, the goddess of divine energy

Antarpaat – a cloth used to shield the arrival of the bride from the groom

Athanu – a general name for pickles

Baath – plain boiled/steamed rice

Babu – pet name for baby son

Badam nu dhudh – milk with ground almonds, sugar and ground cardamom

Barfi – a traditional Indian sweet made with milk, sugar and spices

Bateta nu shaak – potato curry

Besharam – shameless

Bhai – brother

Bhajan – Hindu hymn

Bhajia – fritters made using gram flour and vegetables

Bhakri – leavened thick bread baked on a griddle, made from wheat flour

Bombay sandwiches – a toasted sandwich made with tomatoes, cheese, onions, boiled potatoes and coriander chutney and a special spice blend

Boondi na ladwa – fried bead-sized gram flour balls, steeped in sugar syrups

Brahmin – a Hindu priest

Bus bus – just enough

Chaas – diluted natural yoghurt drink

Chai – brewed tea with milk, sugar and spices

Chakri – fried savoury spirals made out of rice flour and spices

Chana nu shaak – chickpea curry

Chaniya choli – traditional long skirt and blouse worn with a long scarf

Cheda chedi – tying of the groom's and bride's clothes during the wedding

Chevdo – a fried savoury snack made from gram flour noodles, nuts and potato chips, also known as Bombay mix

Chundadi – a scarf worn with chaniya choli or salwaar/churidar kameez

Churidar – tight silk/cotton trouser worn under kameez or sherwani

Dadi – paternal grandmother

Dall – split lentil soups and stews

Dandiya Raas – traditional Gujarati folk dance using short wooden stick

Dhoti – a cloth wrapped around hip and thigh with one end tucked in the back to create baggy trousers

Dikri – a pet name for a daughter

Dikro – pet name for son

Divo – a lamp created using a cotton wick and clarified butter

Diwali – festival of lights to celebrate the return of Rama from exile

Durga puja – a Bengali festival that starts on the 6th day of Navratri

Faiba – paternal aunt

Farali chevdo – fried snack made with tapioca flakes, nuts and potato crisps

Fiaba – paternal aunt

Gajjar no halwo – a carrot, cashew nut and creamy milk pudding.

Garba/garbo – traditional Gujarati folk dance performed during Navratri and festivities

Garchoru – unique wedding saree given to the bride by the groom's family

Gaur keri nu athanu – sweet mango pickle using spices and raw cane sugar

Gulab jamboo – deep fried milk powder and dough balls in sweet sticky rose syrup

Gup shup – in this instance, gossip used mockingly

Haan – yes

Handvo – a savoury lentil cake made from rice, toover dall, and vegetables, baked in the oven

Hastamelap – placing together of the bride's and groom's right hands

Hu tamane batavis – in this instance, I'll show you

Jabo – long shirt worn by men

Jabo pyjamas – long shirt and trousers worn by men

Jaimala – fresh flower garland placed on bride and groom's necks by each other

Jinga curry – spicy curry cooked with king prawns

Jinki dikri – pet name meaning "little daughter"

Kachori – a fried round short pastry ball stuffed with peas or mung dall

Kada – a thick bangle

Kadhi – a thick broth made from gram flour and yoghurt

Kameez – long shirt/dress worn over trousers traditionally worn by women

Kamwari – a woman/girl servant

Kandoro – a jewelled belt worn on the waist over a saree, it usually has bells on it to ward off evil

Kanyadan – the ceremony of giving away of the daughter at marriages

Karela – bitter gourd

Kediyu – a long-sleeeved pleated top worn by men in Gujarat, usually with a dhoti

Keema mattar – minced lamb with peas
Khaman dhokla – a steamed cake made with gram flour and spices
Kheer – creamy rice pudding with cardamon and saffron
Kitchi – steamed rice flour dumplings
Krishna – the most popular deity of Hinduism, he is the eighth avatar of Vishnu
Kurta – long shirt worn by men
Ladli dikri – in this instance, favourite daughter
Luchi – a fried wheat flat bread
Lungi – a long piece of cloth wrapped around the waist, resembles a wrap skirt
Luv shuv – in this instance, the word "love" used mockingly
Mama – maternal uncle
Mami – maternal uncle's wife
Mandap – a four-posted canopy under which a Hindu wedding service is conducted
Mandir – Hindu temple
Mangalphera – the steps around Agni Dev
Mangalsutra – meaning "sacred thread", a gold and black bead necklace given to the bride by the groom
Mara – my
Mara bachulyia – in this instance, my babies
Masa – maternal aunt's husband
Masala Chai – brewed tea with milk, sugar and spices like cardamom, cinnamon, ginger
Masi – maternal aunt, a term used for aunty in general
Mattar baath – fried and steamed rice and peas
Mehndi – paste of crushed leaves of the henna plant used to create intricate body art during weddings and festivals
Methi chicken – chicken curry with fenugreek seeds

Mishti doi – a sweetened natural yogurt dish from Bengal

Mutton biryani – pilau rice, layered with mutton, vegetables and rice, cooked slowly in the oven

Nana – maternal grandfather

Nani – maternal grandmother

Nasto – savoury snacks

Navratri – nine-day festival to celebrate the divine power of the goddess Durga

Navratri ni adham – the eighth day of Navratri

Nazar lage jase – in this instance, she will get bad luck

Pallu – the decorated end of a saree that is left loose or displayed at the front

Paneer – a fresh cheese

Panetar – white and red saree worn by a Gujarati bride, given to her by a maternal uncle

Papad – thin crispy bread made with lentil or rice flour eaten either fried or dry-roasted on flame

Pari – angel

Parotha – griddle-fried layered flatbread made from wheat flour and cooked with ghee

Pau bhaji – fried bread rolls with mashed spiced vegetables and butter

Penda – traditional Indian sweet made with milk, sugar and spices

Puri – deep-fried small, rolled flatbread made from wheat flour

Puttar – pet name for a child in Punjabi

Radha Krishna – the feminine and masculine manifestation of god

Rahu – freshwater fish eaten as delicacy, similar to carp

Rajkotya – people who come from the town of Rajkot, Gujarat

Ringda nu shaak – aubergine curry

Ringda ne valor nu shaak – aubergine and hyacinth beans curry

Rotla – thick, soft bread baked on griddle pan made with millet flour

Rotli – thinly rolled wheat rounds baked on a griddle pan

Samosa – triangular potato-and-pea stuffed fried pastry

Sanji – song and dance ceremony also known as sandhya sangeet

Saree – traditional garment worn by Indian women

Saree blouse – a short matching or contrasting top worn with a long skirt or saree

Sasara – in this instance, in-laws

Septapadi – seven vows performed at a Hindu wedding

Shaak – any vegetable curry

Sherwani – a long coat that is worn by the groom

Sindoor – a vermilion red pigment used in Hindu ceremonies and worn by a married Hindu woman

Sondesh – traditional Bengali sweet made with paneer, milk, sugar and spices

Tame kaya gham na cho – what town are you from

Thepla – griddle-fried wheat flour and gram flour thinly rolled bread

Tika – an ornament worn on the forehead by women

Tilak – auspicious mark on the forehead using vermilion or sandalwood

Tusi great ho Uncleji, Sat Shri Akaal – you're great uncle, God is great

Vahu – daughter in law

Vaishnav – followers of the many avatars of Vishnu

Vichitra manus – strange man

Vidaai – the final ceremony of the Hindu weeding, when the bride leaves her maternal home

Hema's Handvo Recipe

This savoury lentil cake made from rice, toover dall, and vegetables, is baked in the oven and is a firm favourite in all Gujarati households. It is often made for brunch or picnics. Hema uses courgettes instead of bottle gourd (dhoodhi) in this recipe. Other families add cabbage, carrots, peas and peanuts too.

Ingredients

2 cups of basmati rice
1 cup of toover dall
¼ cup of urad dall
¼ cup of mung dall
¼ cup of chana dall
1 cup of sour natural yoghurt
2 cups of grated courgette (instead of dhoodhi)
1 cup of chopped onions
1 tablespoon grated ginger
1 tablespoon minced green chillies
3 tablespoons of finely chopped fresh coriander
9 tablespoons of sunflower oil
2 tablespoons of wholewheat flour
Juice of half a lemon
2 teaspoons of sugar
1 to 2 teaspoons of salt
1 teaspoon of soda bicarbonate
1 teaspoon of garlic paste
1 teaspoon red chilli powder
½ teaspoon of turmeric
2 teaspoons of mustard seeds
2 teaspoons of cumin seeds
1 small stick of cassia bark

3-4 cloves
2-3 dried red chillies
2 tablespoons of sesame seeds
½ teaspoon of asafoetida
3-4 curry leaves

Method
Wash and soak the rice and pulses overnight in plenty of warm water, you may need to top this up, making sure to keep the mixture moist.

Add the yoghurt and grind the rice and pulse to a coarse paste the consistency of thick batter. Add one tablespoon of oil and wheat flour and mix thoroughly. Cover and leave to ferment for 3 - 4 hours in a warm place.

Preheat the oven to 180 Centigrade.

Squeeze out the water from the courgette using a muslin cloth or clean tea towel.

Mix the chilli, ginger, grated courgette, garlic, salt, sugar, turmeric, 4 tablespoons of oil, lemon juice and soda bicarbonate (if you want the handvo to be even lighter add the Eno here), mix well and spread the mixture in a greased baking tin.

In a small frying pan, heat 5 tablespoons of oil and add the mustard, cumin seeds, cassia bark and cloves. When the seeds pop, add the curry leaves, asafoetida, chopped onions and sesame seeds. Take the pan off the heat and pour the heated oil over the batter.

Bake in the oven for 30 - 40 minutes, the handvo should be golden brown. Check it's cooked through by inserting a skewer in the centre. It should come out dry.

Serve like a cake with masala chai for brunch or try it with a cool glass of chaas..

Acknowledgement

I cannot write this without mentioning the pandemic. It has left many unable to write and many to create more and more work. I am probably one of those that used this time to write, to escape. I wrote the outline for this book straight after I published my debut duets, *My Heart Sings Your Song* and *Where Have We Come.* It was an idea that came to me as I read *Rebecca* again. I can't remember how many times I keep going back to the book by Daphne du Maurier, but it is a favourite I pick up often. Du Maurier's novel has many similarities to *Jane Eyre,* the protagonist feels unloved and unworthy, both are orphans and full of suspicion with affection yet have an independent streak that shows through their life choices. However, the pandemic made putting pen to paper and the reworking of the idea difficult. I wrote lots of short stories which I hope to publish and share with you eventually, but longer work kept getting stuck in the muddled middle. So this novel has gone back and forth often to reach the finish line. I hope you like it as much as I enjoyed the final version.

There may only be one author listed in this book, but I couldn't have written it without the support and constant encouragement of my family and friends. To my beta readers and my early support team, your feedback, support, and constant friendship are more than I deserve. Thank you all for allowing me to fulfil my dream of writing stories. If you want to join my Beta team, please drop me an email. You'll get a chance to read my book before the tweaks and changes and contribute to making me a better writer.

To Hassy & JM whose house in South of France inspired the setting for this book. And for correcting my French dialogue. I look forward to going back to Aix and walk along The Barrage.

To Shaylin and Claire for your excellent editing and proofreading.

To my family: my constant—you've been through my life's tribulations and helped me tremendously. I don't say it often enough, but you are my rock and I love you always. My life would be empty without you.

To all the Bollywood films I have watched and loved for giving me inspiration for some of the dialogue, I have taken liberties with the translation of the lyrics in the songs that I've quoted, so for those of you who are fluent in Hindi and Urdu forgive me.

To the old Hollywood films, I've watched especially *Jane Eyre*, 1943, Orson Welles, Jane Fontaine, Robert Stevenson and *Rebecca* 1940, Laurence Olivier, Jane Fontaine, Alfred Hitchcock. There's a scene in Jane Eyre where Mr Rochester horse startles at meeting Jane on her walk through the dark windy moors. That scene has made my heart tremble many times. I hope I captured that meeting in my reworking of it with Hema and Rahul's meeting.

To all the authors who have inspired me, Bronte's *Jane Eyre* is a character I return to often. Her depiction of Jane as an independent and spirited woman who seeks someone to love is remarkably modern and is worth reading if you haven't read it. For me it is a coming of age story, of finding your identity and being happy. I am a reader first and foremost. Last year more than any other I have discovered many new authors, especially stories that have helped me discover new worlds to escape to, whether real or imaginary.

Finally, and most importantly to you, my readers, THANK YOU so much for reading my story, I hope you liked it. I am always interested in connecting with you, via social media or email.

Please leave a review; it will help other readers find new stories and help self-published author like me to reach new readers. If you leave a review and send me a screen shot email details on my contact page. I'll send you a unique chapter from Rahul's perspective, and while you're there sign up to my newsletter, where I'll share recipes, short stories and news of new books. **sazvora.com**

Reading Group Guide

1. Music has a significant role in how Rahul deals with his emotions. Do certain songs have special meaning for you?

2. So many characters in this book are hiding different aspects of their histories. What do they hide behind? Would sharing their histories ease their heartache?

3. Gayatri and Mukesh find love later in life but are afraid of upsetting their children. Do you think they were right to wait so long? What advice would you give to them, especially as widow marriage is frowned upon in their community?

4. Chanda treats Hema badly, and this has put a strain on their relationship. Do you think that she should have been more patient and caring for Hema? Hema falls in love with Amelie easily. Do you think it is easy to love a child you care for?

5. Madeleine and Céleste help Rajni meet with her child Amelie. Do you think they were right to help her?

6. Niraj and Hema are introduced to each other because of their disability. Do you think it was right for Dennis to find a disabled suitor for his cousin?

7. Both Hema and Rahul believe they have found someone special. Do you believe in soul mates?

8. Rahul employs Hema. Do you think it was wise of Rahul to ask her to be his tennis partner?

9. The age difference between Rahul and Hema creates a barrier. Do you think the age difference between two people in love matters?

10. Jane Eyre by Charlotte Bronte inspires this story. Does it stay true to the original?

About the Author

Saz Vora is a wife, mother and writer. She was born in East Africa and migrated with her family in the '60s to Coventry, Midlands, where she grew up straddling British and Gujarati Indian culture. Her debut novels, *My Heart Sings Your Song* and *Where Have We Come* is a story in two parts of love, life, family, conflict, and two young people striving to remain together throughout. *Where Have We Come*, Finalist - The Wishing Shelf 2020, is based on true events that have shaped her outlook on life's trials and tribulations. Her short story *Broad Street Library* was long listed in The Spread Word, Life Writing Prize 2020.

Before she started writing South Asian melodrama, she had a successful career in Television Production and Teaching… But her need to write stories has led to what she is doing now – writing stories about people like me in multi-cultural Britain.

She gets inspiration from listening to music, cooking and watching Bollywood, Hollywood and Independent films, hence the references to songs, food and films in all my books.

Her books are stories that make you think, for readers who like the multicultural layers of South Asian family drama, especially using storytelling to tell women's stories on taboo issues. She draws on my upbringing in England and the layers of complexity of living with my Indian heritage and my Britishness.

Find out more through her blog **sazvora.com**

Books by Saz

University Series
Reena and Nikesh

My Heart Sings Your Song Book One

When Reena met Nikesh, her head told her to keep away from the wealthy, charming playboy, but her heart had other plans. But Nikesh's persistence won her over, and she thought she'd found her Bollywood style happily ever after, despite their different backgrounds.

During the summer holiday, Nikesh disappeared when Reena needs him most.
Can she avoid bumping into him when they go back to finish their final year? Will he try to get her to give him a second chance? Or has Sarladevi found him a suitable girl?

Where Have We Come Book Two

At the birth of their first child Reena and Nikesh discover their baby has had a severe brain haemorrhage, and family and friends rally around to help. But the family matriarch, Sarladevi, reminds Reena of the predictions of the Guru and Reena struggles to deal with her past.

Will the chasm created by their differences in dealing with the stresses and strains of looking after a sick child pull them apart? Or will their love for each other and the eternal love of their child overcome the prejudices and customs observed by Nik's family?

Search and scan on Spotify for my playlist.

Lightning Source UK Ltd.
Milton Keynes UK
UKHW010755160921
390677UK00001B/179

9 781838 146528